Praise for

Cheat Sheets

When I first read Edward O'Dwyer's incredible poetry collection, *Bad News, Good News, Bad News*, I wondered how he'd ever top it. Then he goes and comes up with *Cheat Sheets*, an astonishing collection of vignettes about life, love, lust and relationships, which are jaw-droppingly hilarious, tender, strange, potent and weirdly charming— all at the same time. I laughed out loud in public too many times, the laughs often interrupted with sharp intakes of breath, as stories took outrageously i-didn't-see-that-coming turns. If there isn't yet a law against this much talent in one single human, then there ought to be. Move over Dan Rhodes. If I have any advice for readers when they sit down with this collection, it is this: pace yourself. Like a packet of Nestlé's Rolos or a family size packet of salt & vinegar crisps, you won't want these stories to end.

~ Ali Whitelock, author of *and my heart crumples like a coke can* and *Poking seaweed with a stick and running away from the smell*

Disturbingly knowing and knowingly disturbing, Edward O'Dwyer comes at his delicate subject matter with a playful and razor eye. These are shards that insist on being read, and then read again.

~ Alan McMonagle, author of *Psychotic Episodes*
and *Ithaca*

Cheat Sheets explores infidelity with a wry and clever wit. It is a side-splitting study on the absurdity of human behaviour.

~ Tanya Farrelly, author of *The Girl Behind the Lens*
and *When Black Dogs Sing*

Congratulations on this collection. These are wicked little gems! Each one was a treat to read.

~ Donal Ryan, author of *The Spinning Heart* and
From a Low and Quiet Sea

CHEAT SHEETS

EDWARD O'DWYER

TRUTH SERUM PRESS

Truth Serum Press
32 Meredith Street
Sefton Park SA 5083
Australia

Email: truthserumpress@live.com.au
Website: https://truthserumpress.net
Truth Serum Press catalogue: https://truthserumpress.net/catalogue/

Original front cover photograph copyright © StockSnap
Original back cover photograph copyright © Gabriel Ferraz
Author photo by Shane Vaughan
Cover design copyright © Matt Potter

ISBN: 978-1-925536-60-7

Also available as an eBook
ISBN: 978-1-925536-61-4

Truth Serum Press is a member of the
Bequem Publishing collective
https://www.bequempublishing.com/

for

Avril and Brendan Kirrane

Introduction

The following is a collection of very short fictions, all of them dark comedies with the unifying theme of infidelity. Each one outlines a situation of dreadful romantic betrayal, and always in comically exaggerated and outlandish detail.

I had a lot of fun coming up with the most bizarre situations I possibly could, and then stretching out the boundaries of likelihood as far as they would go. Mind you, some of these things just might be close enough to somebody's truth. I've already found that out during one particular public reading and, thankfully, she was seeing the funny side of it.

What to expect: lashings of farce, surrealism, quirkiness, invention, cunning, a whole load of scandalous behaviour, and a generous helping of incredibly daft antics. You can expect to laugh out loud. You can even, sometimes, expect to worry about the status of your immortal soul when you do laugh. That's all part of the fun of it. It's all part of what the book is about.

The book owes a debt to the work of English writer Dan Rhodes. When I read his books, I was blown away by their unique brand of dark humour and imaginative possibility. I kept thinking: why don't more books like these exist? From there I decided to have a go at writing a book that might find a place in that category, and so here we are.

From there I just needed a theme to give focus to the writing, something both universal and pertinent, and with a near-limitless potential for both big laugh moments and, just as importantly, wry chuckle moments.

Then, two women sitting at the next table to me in a café one afternoon were chatting loudly about the affair one of them was having. I didn't have any choice but to overhear. There was a time people would speak in hushed tones for this kind of thing, but the utter casualness of it was alarming and, I felt, also significant in a broad, cultural sense, as very little seems to be taboo anymore. Well, that was that: I had my theme.

Before you dive into the suffering and cruelty and idiocy of these characters, I should say that any resemblance to real life in these stories is absolutely coincidental. One further disclaimer: the author does not endorse or encourage the behaviour of any of these awful, philandering sinners, but definitely does encourage laughter at them, as well as sharing their escapades with friends, family, work colleagues and, from time to time, strangers.

Edward O'Dwyer, June 2018

Contents

1

"I can resist everything except temptation."

Oscar Wilde
from *Lady Windermere's Fan*

Dolls

I came upon my daughter sitting on the living room floor playing with her dolls. Sitting down to observe her, I hoped to hear that wonderful giggle that melts my heart every time.

"What are your dolls' names?" I asked her.

"This is Mommy and this is Daddy," she answered, raising the two figures she was holding in her hands.

"And who is that one?" I asked, nodding towards the third doll, which was by her side and had a big head of blonde hair, and was wearing a bright pink cocktail dress.

"Oh," she said. "That's Daddy's girlfriend."

"Daddy has a girlfriend?" I gasped, not quite sure if I was hearing her correctly. Suddenly I was feeling a great worry come over me. Relax, I told myself, there is no way she could know anything. This was just a case of kids and their imaginations, nothing more.

"Yes," she said. "Mommy has just found out and now she and Daddy are arguing." At that point I had to get up and leave the room. I could feel perspiration appearing on my forehead. Stay calm, I thought. There's no problem here, none. Neither my wife nor daughter could have any clue about the other woman I've been seeing. It's just pure coincidence, that's all. She probably just saw something on TV and thought to re-enact it.

When I'd regained control of myself and fanned my brow sufficiently, I mustered the courage to go back to the living room, and hoped, once more, to hear that wonderful giggle I'd first entered the room for.

"So, what's happening now?" I asked her. That's when I noticed that Daddy's head had come away from the rest of his body.

"Mommy told Daddy's girlfriend that he's already married," she answered.

"Oh, what a mess!" I said. "And how did she take that?" That's when she picked up the headless doll and waved it about in front of me.

"Not very well," she answered. "They decided to work together to kill Daddy." At that moment, my breezy calmness, I was sure, was no more. I could feel all the colour draining from my face and, at that, she threw her arms around me. "It's okay, Daddy," she said, "don't feel bad. They're only dolls."

Blindness

I had a wandering eye and my wife has always been the jealous type. You can imagine all the silly rows we had.

"It's just looking. It's harmless," I'd protest. "I would never, ever act on it."

"It's not harmless," she'd reply. "It's cheating. I see the way you look at other women and you might as well be sleeping with them when you look at them like that."

I couldn't help myself, and after each argument continued looking at beautiful women and licking my lips. I even sometimes looked at ordinary women and licked my lips.

Then she decided she'd had enough, and replaced my eye drops with hydrochloric acid and, of course, I lost my vision quite painfully.

"I know you get jealous, but this is just too far," I told her afterwards. "You really are lucky I love you so much, otherwise I would leave you."

"You'd never leave me," she said, and took my hands in hers, putting a stop to their poking and prodding at my sightless eyes. "I knew there was no risk of it." I felt her kiss tenderly on my cheek and accepted the truth of what she was saying.

She has been so wonderful all these years about my blindness. She never loses patience with me when I stumble into a wall or break an ornament around the house. She guides me through the streets, reads menus aloud; everything you can think of that a blind man can't do for himself. She even took a creative writing class so that she could effectively and poetically describe sunsets and such things to me. I really don't know what I would do without her.

Yesterday was the tenth anniversary of my blindness and, as I do each year, I thanked her for it. Just like she has done all the previous years, she told me I was more than welcome.

"I've never, ever been happier," I said.

"I haven't either," she replied. "And to think, I very nearly chickened out of doing it."

Cinema

I met a real beauty of a girl and she agreed to go out with me. I took her to the cinema because it takes the pressure off and then later, over a drink or two, you at least have the movie to talk about.

During the film I slid my hand over onto a knee and gave it a small squeeze, as you do. Soon she was grabbing my face and kissing me senseless. We kissed for the entirety of the movie until the lights came on and it was time to leave.

Just how long a film was that, I wondered. I was looking at my date and she had aged terribly during it. She could easily have passed for mid-eighties now. She was looking at me and smiling, her lipstick smudged all over her face.

Then I remembered the beauty I had come in with had been sitting on the other side of me. I turned around but she was gone. She must have given up on the film when she heard all the distracting smooching noises coming from beside her. I felt awful for her, especially having insisted she pay for the tickets.

Boost

I arrived home to discover my wife naked and handcuffed to our bed. Things had become a little stale between us and we had agreed we needed to do something about it, something to put the spark back into that side of things. I'd even been worried that if we didn't find a solution soon she might give up and start having affairs.

I had to hand it to her. I had to give her huge credit for daring such a bold effort to spice things up. She hadn't ever been one for kinky stuff. This was a whole new side to her and I was instantly excited by it. I heard the toilet flush then in the *en suite* bathroom and, a moment later, a naked and very fit looking man came out of there. I felt my mouth fall open with horror at the sight of him. It wasn't that I had never fantasised about having a threesome, of course. What man hasn't? Like most, I just always imagined it would be with two beautiful women. She had gone to all this effort, though, and I really didn't want to seem ungrateful by pointing it out. It just wouldn't be fair at all. I looked at her stretched out in the bed and saw a terrible panic in her face.

Bless her, she was probably so nervous about all of this and there was I keeping her waiting on some sign that I was happy with it all. I couldn't bear to let her down, and so forced myself to begin undressing.

"You really are wonderful to come up with all of this," I told her, making deep eye contact, determined that it would give our love life just the boost it needed.

Special

I tell my favourite girlfriend she is the only one for me, because I want her to understand that she is very special. I feel so very blessed to call her my girlfriend, and naturally want her to be in no doubt about her importance. I would never, ever say the same of my other two girlfriends, but that isn't to say I am not pleased with them. On the contrary, they are both wonderful. It's just that some people really deserve to be set apart, don't you think? Some people really do earn the pedestals we put them on.

Ring

I received word that my wife had been kidnapped and if I ever wanted to see her again I'd better pay the accompanying ransom. The same note also mentioned that if I contacted the police they would know it and kill her immediately in a very painful fashion.

Days passed of thinking about what I should do before, finally, I opted to simply disregard it, balling up the note and tossing it on the flames of the roaring fire I'd just set for my date that evening. I'd been seeing another woman for a while before all of this, and now I was leaning towards asking her to become my girlfriend on an official capacity. My heart was beating fast with excitement at the thought, and that was even before I'd realised we could have full use of the Jacuzzi without any worry at all that my wife might arrive home and discover us there.

Becoming impatient, my wife's kidnappers sent further word that they were not kidding around at all and that soon they would be sending bits of her through the mail. It was too late, though, my mind was made up. I ripped up the note into little bits and threw the bunch of paper flecks in the bin.

True to their word, soon a parcel arrived and it was her wedding band finger, and still wearing the ring, unusually. Perhaps they were trying to prove beyond any doubt that it was indeed my wife's finger, but I couldn't help thinking it a very silly move on their part, since the ring is genuine diamond and worth many, many thousands. They weren't at all cut out for this kidnapping business – that much was clear.

It was all working out very well. I could hardly believe my good fortune. I stuffed the stiff, ghastly finger in the garbage disposal, then cleaned the ring and stored it safely away. After all, I figured I might need it again soon enough.

Congratulations

I couldn't quite decide upon the best way to tell my wife the truth, but one thing was for sure, it was time to put a stop to the lies.

I racked my brains and, in the end, picked up a Hallmark card from one of the shops in town. It was for somebody who'd passed their exams. There was a picture of a very cute cartoon dog looking delighted with himself while wearing a graduate cloak and tossing his cap into the air.

"Congratulations, you've passed!" it said in big, glittery letters.

On the inside was where I wrote my confession. "I've been having an affair," I began, "and am leaving you for good, and I'm not particularly sorry for it." I figured it was best to get straight to the point.

She never did go to university and hadn't recently done exams of any description, so she would have been confused by the card initially, I'm sure, but I hoped it might somehow soften the blow. I mean, that dog is just so chuffed, how could anyone not smile?

It must go back to how I was brought up. I was taught that if you have to give somebody bad news, break it to them as gently as you can.

Devil

I was alone in a bar and got chatting to a woman who wasn't my wife. No good was going to come of it, but resisting her wouldn't be easy, such was her beauty, her slinky red dress accentuating sinfully perfect curves.

When she excused herself to go to the bathroom, it was my chance to leave with no harm done, but then I felt a small weight appear on my shoulder. When I turned my head there was a little devil standing there, his horned red face grinning fiendishly at me. I looked down and saw tiny hoofs instead of feet, and he had the cutest little trident clasped in his hands.

"How can you be thinking of leaving?" he asked. "I think she really likes you, and a woman like that doesn't come along every day. You should forget about your wife for tonight. Go for it."

Just then a similarly small weight appeared on my other shoulder. When I turned my head to see what it was, sure enough, there was a little angel standing there. He had a tiny golden halo hovering over his head and on his back were the most elegant little pair of white-feathered wings.

"Oh thank God you're here," I blurted out. "You have to tell me what to do." I knew time was of the essence. She would be back from the bathroom any moment.

"Well, normally I would tell you to do the opposite of what the other guy said," he began. "He's right, though, she is really hot, definitely an example of His very best work. I'm pretty sure I'm going to get into a lot of trouble for this, but I have to agree. You should forget about your wife for tonight. Go for it."

Bus

My girlfriend and I got on the bus but unfortunately there weren't two seats together available, so we were forced to sit with strangers. Though only a few feet away, soon I missed her terribly, so I turned around and smiled at her and she smiled back at me.

Not long after that, I was missing her again, and even more intensely than the time before. Unfortunately she didn't notice when I swung around to smile at her again. This time she had her head turned and was deep in conversation with the very good-looking man sitting next to her.

The next time I was missing her intensely, I turned around to smile once more at her but on this occasion found that they were kissing very passionately and with very busy hands.

Suddenly the bus crashed and all its passengers were thrown from their seats into the air. When I regained consciousness I realised immediately I was losing blood fast from a few orifices. There was a grotesque mess of broken and bent bodies all around me.

I turned back to see my girlfriend, not to smile at her but in hope that she'd not been hurt. She and the man had been thrown into the aisle and her body was on top of his. They both looked in urgent need of medical attention. I could see that a part of his skull had become exposed by some terrible impact, and she had somehow been speared all the way through her stomach by somebody's umbrella, which had then opened up above them, probably because the activation button had caught on one of her internal organs.

Quite amazingly, they remained kissing each other every bit as exuberantly as before. It was as if they hadn't even noticed what was happening.

Ocean

My husband found out I've secretly had a pen-pal in Argentina for the last twenty years, with whom I've been exchanging only erotic letters, detailed accounts of the most debauched sexual fantasies. It was exciting and yet innocent, I've always felt, since there was an ocean and several thousands of miles between us anyway. There was certainly no cause for my husband to worry.

He found the letters and isn't taking it well at all. He's been reading them for the past few days now, sobbing uncontrollably all the while. I think he intends to read every one of them, which means he could be at it for weeks more. By the time he's done there could be an ocean between us and I'll have to find the time to write to him as well.

Yellow

for Jack O'Donnell

Work takes me out of the country quite a bit, and I miss my wife terribly, but we make the best of it. We *Facetime* each night I'm away. It makes it so much more bearable, being so far away, when I know that I will still be able to see her pretty face and hear her melodious voice.

Last night, however, I couldn't help noticing the pair of men's underwear hanging from a corner of the picture frame behind her head. It certainly wasn't one of mine, I could tell right away, what with them being fluorescent yellow. She was sipping a glass of red wine, seemingly unaware of them.

I didn't know what to say, whether to point their presence out to her or not.

"Are you okay, honey?" she asked. "You seem a little distracted."

"It's just been a tough day," I said. "I'm shattered, that's all." I wrapped the call up pretty quickly by faking several large yawns and claiming that I'd a very early start in the morning. I was panicking. Was there any conceivable way this could be innocent?

The image of her wild, passionate, love-making face flashed in my mind, followed by the image of her hand recklessly tossing the underwear into the air.

I really had to be up early so tried to get some sleep, knowing it wouldn't be easy. It was impossible, as it turns out. I didn't get a wink. Every time I closed my eyes all I could see was fluorescent yellow.

Serious

"When are you going to get serious?" she asked, her voice with that had-it-up-to-here-with-you quality so many women are experts at. This was a few years ago, and the question had taken me by surprise in a big way. I had felt sure then that all aspects of our relationship were great.

I suddenly began living in fear of losing her, and made a conscientious effort to stop making all the silly jokes it occurred to me to make, hoping that this would please her. I got a complete new wardrobe, very austere, sensible ensembles, greys and beiges, nothing garish. I applied for a promotion at work, and got it, with a handsome increase in salary and benefits, including a fancy company car.

There were plenty more long evenings to put in at the office, but the way I saw it, each one reaffirmed just how deadly serious I'd become. How could she not be very, very impressed?

I arrived home a little earlier than expected one evening, and thought to pick up some flowers and a good French wine on the way. When I entered the living room, thinking to find her there, there was only a clown sat drinking a can of beer, starkers naked but for the elaborate makeup on his face, a plastic red nose, and some big, floppy shoes. He was grinning from ear to ear at me.

"Listen, honey, this really isn't at all what it looks like," she began to explain after arriving through the other door, from the kitchen, and finding me there. She quickly gave up, though, seeing by the pain on my face that I wasn't about to be fooled by any flimsy excuse.

"I'm so sorry," she gasped, "it's just that you've become so serious over the past few years. I do still love you, but the man I fell in love with was just so much fun." The clown, still sitting there on our sofa with his genitals exposed, took a long, noisy swig of his beer, watching us, grinning.

"I mean, take now, for instance," she went on. "You just look so bloody serious."

2

"The guys with girlfriends never told Rebecca they had girlfriends until after they had slept with her. Maybe they detected some moral strain in her, some impetus to protect girlfriends. Maybe they detected the opposite, and were thus protecting their girlfriends from Rebecca."

Rebecca Schiff
from 'Third Person' in
The Bed Moved

Rollercoaster

She was meant to be the girl I married, the woman I spent the rest of my life making happy. I felt it from Day One, and soon she told me she wouldn't look at another man ever again, but that turned out to be a lie.

"I'm sorry," she gasped, "but I've just seen the man of my dreams. I never thought it could be like this." We were on a rollercoaster at the time, and she was pointing. As we whizzed by I saw the blurry shape of a man and wondered how this could have been the man of her dreams. "I'm sure you'll hate me for this," she went on, "but I've just gotta do what I've gotta do."

With superhuman strength, she snapped off the safety barrier holding us in place and threw it aside and leapt from the contraption. It was the worst time to do so as we were at the apex of the track's height. I suppose she just couldn't wait, and had maybe noticed the blurry shape of the man she'd pointed at had begun to walk away in the opposite direction.

When the ride came to its end, I raced over to the forming crowd and shoved my way to the front. "I'm her boyfriend," I yelled, knowing, either way, it would be the last day I'd have to utter these words of her.

As I looked down at the gruesome mess of her, I knew it was too late. Her body was bent in ways not even circus performers should ever hope to bend. Her head had cracked open against the concrete and spilled its contents for all to see. I'd always joked affectionately that if she had brains she'd be dangerous, but I never meant it seriously. I really didn't find it in any way funny, and yet, looking at the grey, gloopy matter, I could feel a smirk forcing itself across my face.

Friend

At first I was thrilled when my wife and best friend got along as well as they did. You often see cases where one is jealous of the other and then the poor guy stuck in the middle is put in the position where he has to choose between them all the time. I even got precious time to myself when they started doing things just the two of them.

Unfortunately, though, they got along so famously, it wasn't long before she left me for him. She moved out of the house and weeks went by without seeing or hearing from her. When she turned up at the door with a nervous smile on her face, though, I couldn't hold back my happiness.

"You've come back to me!" I yelled, my voice high-pitched with excitement.

"Ha, very funny," she said. "But seriously, do you mind if I just have a quick look behind the bed? I think a pair of handcuffs might have fallen behind there."

"But we never used any handcuffs in bed," I pointed out.

"I know," she said, letting out a weary sigh. "Now do you mind if I go check? It'll only take a second."

Kids

My wife was sleeping with other men. I'd been suspicious for a while but did all I could to convince myself I was being paranoid, insecure. Some signs are difficult to ignore, though, and when I confronted her about it, she came clean.

"As angry and betrayed as I'm feeling now," I told her, "we're going to get through this. I know we will. We have to. We owe it to ourselves but especially to the kids."

"We're not going to get through this," she replied. She put a soft hand on my cheek and then looked deeply into my eyes. "I'm afraid we're going to be getting a divorce. It might even be a good idea to look into having some paternity tests done."

Practical

My girlfriend is very practical. She has it all worked out. She has graphs for this and pie charts for that. She has calculated all the probabilities and told me that, within an acceptable margin of error, she's satisfied I'll make a reliable and solid, if unspectacular, husband. I will be an excellent provider with one more promotion, and will make an attentive, nurturing father.

Therefore, she has informed me that she will strongly consider a marriage proposal from me. In all of this she made no mention of love, but as I said, she is very practical. I love her very much and so, of course, dream of one day making her my wife.

I have a ring picked out and have applied for that promotion and am just waiting to hear from them, although I'm quietly confident of it. If I do get it, I'll give her the news and my new salary figures and then get down on one knee. That's the plan. I figure it will be very practical and she'll love it and have to say yes.

She did mention one problem. She has said that I leave a lot to be desired when it comes to the bedroom. It's the only thing really letting me down as a marriage prospect. I took it purely as constructive criticism because she is so very practical.

"It isn't a deal-breaker," she reassured me. "I can always have affairs," she joked. At least I hoped she was joking. Sometimes it isn't easy to know.

"That won't be necessary, I'm quite certain I can improve," I replied, meaning to do whatever it took to do so. I'm sure I can. If there's one thing I've learned from our being together it's that there is a practical solution to every problem.

Nurse

While having my appendix removed, I spent a week being pampered by nurses and discovered I had a thing for that. I told my wife about it soon after, handing her an *Ann Summers* bag and excitedly urging her to open it.

"That's disgusting," she said, twisting up her face as she held the PVC nurse's uniform up in front of her. "You're to bring this back to the shop first thing in the morning, and then never mention this fetish again," and she said the word 'fetish' as though she would have to leave the conversation there to go and take a shower immediately.

I didn't give up, however. Having stored the uniform away, I brought it up several more times, but unfortunately, each time without any more success than the last.

On the way home from work one day, I had an impulse to crash the car into a wall at a moderate speed. I can't say what possessed me, but I received only minor injuries and was feeling very thrilled with myself as the ambulance took me away to be among all those pretty nurses at the hospital again. I imagined they were going to spoil me exceptionally this time, since I might have been killed if I'd been going faster.

Sure enough, they were everything I remembered, and more.

When my wife arrived to see me, she was quite distraught. She was so relieved, however, to discover my injuries weren't very serious, and that I'd make a full recovery and be back home soon enough. I felt the sting of those words and figured I'd soon have to come up with another reason to be brought in here.

"Don't you ever scare me like that again," she said, hugging me to her. "I don't know what I'd do without you; now I want you to promise me you'll never scare me like that again. Promise me!"

"I can't promise anything, my love," I answered, smiling at her, "but I think it's time we talk a bit about how we might minimise the risk."

Denial

Yesterday, my girlfriend revealed to me that she's a nymphomaniac. I suppose the signs were there, and not realising it before must have been due to a great deal of denial. She's had sex with over 500 other men, as it turns out, and that's just in the time we've been together.

"You've no idea how sorry I am," she said. "I would never, ever mean to hurt you, but I can't go on like this. You deserve so much better."

I didn't know how to respond in the moment, but now that I've had a day to think it over, it's very clear what I have to do. I'm just waiting for her to get in from work, and I'm going to tell her that there's nothing at all to forgive, and that I love her so very much that I'm going to become a nymphomaniac as well, so that I will be able to understand exactly what she's going through, and that way we can overcome it together.

Rome

"Where are you taking us this summer?" my husband asks, nudging me with his elbow, grinning at me. Like one of those people quitting swearing by keeping a swear jar, I have to put a euro in a jar for every time I look at another man's groin. It pays for our holidays. He's so amazing, to be able to joke around about it the way he does. He's a saint.

I'm such a terror for it. Honestly, I can't even begin to explain it. And it's any man at all, as well. It isn't just the hunky ones. I'll even look at the most inappropriate ones. I actually looked at my husband's father's groin back when I was meeting him for the first time all those years ago. Yes, that's correct – this has been going on for years.

"Maybe Tenerife," he teases. "Or I hear Croatia's got some incredible beaches."

"I'm sorry," is all I can say. "I'm so very sorry. I don't know what's wrong with me."

"It's okay, love," he says cradling me inside consoling arms. I know that it's far from okay. He's so wonderful that of course I deserve all the shame I feel, and more again. Looking at all these men's groins surely makes me the worst wife in the world. He catches me in the act all the time and then pretends not to. I must be very sick in the head to be carrying on like this.

"Actually, I've always wanted to see Rome," he calls out from the next room, and I can't help myself – I start thinking awful things about the Roman men. They are walking down their ancient streets, all wearing the tightest trousers imaginable, great bulging manhoods threatening to burst out of them. I'm the worst wife ever.

"Okay, Rome sounds wonderful," I call back to him. "Let's go to Rome."

Strangle

I didn't plan to become a serial killer. No, but like a lot of things, it just sort of happens, I suppose. Then, suddenly, you are a serial killer. You're not quite sure how it's happened, but there's no denying it has.

If you have ever made love to my husband during the time we've been together, then you're most likely on my list. I'm coming to get you. Everyone who has been mysteriously killed so far has that one thing in common so, naturally, he became a suspect, but I always take great care to make sure he has a rock-solid alibi. Cheating scoundrel or not, I love him and it wouldn't do to have him sent away to prison.

So yes, I kill only as an act of love. I love him so, so much. It's another thing that, like becoming a serial killer, isn't easily explained. He isn't particularly handsome or sexy, or talented or successful, or charming, and yet I find myself absolutely hooked on him. When he smiles his wonky, gap-toothed smile at me, I feel my knees weaken and become light-headed and sometimes even short of breath.

It's nothing personal, of course, my strangling you. You're not the one who has done wrong here. I'm sure he doesn't admit to being married. Call it bad luck, then, shall we? Nonetheless, you have to die. It isn't negotiable, I'm afraid. I do hope on some level you'll understand, when the time arrives, the great strength in my hands comes wholly out of love and not hate.

Wall

I had no choice but to dump my husband recently. Through our years together we never once discussed politics until that night. When he told me who he'd voted for in the presidential election, I just couldn't go on with it. The marriage was a sham.

"There's a lot I can forgive," I told him, and it's true, I have been a forgiving, self-sacrificing wife. He's had lots of affairs and I got over them all, because I'm also a modern woman, and no modern woman should end her marriage over silly, meaningless affairs. There's nothing more traditional, if you ask me. Instead, I'd just had my own affairs and called it the solution.

"You can't be serious, my love," he protested. "Is it really over?" His voice was a pathetic little whimper. I was wondering what I'd ever seen in him. Suddenly all his flaws were clear to me, things I'd not seemed to take any notice of before, like the weird knobby growth next to his left nostril.

"I'm very serious," I said, "and yes, it is over. I don't mind tolerating your philandering. I don't mind turning a blind eye to that. I'm a modern woman after all, but I have to draw the line somewhere."

He began weeping like a child who'd dropped all his sweets, but I wasn't about to soften towards him, not this time. He'd get no sympathy from me, not with those political leanings.

"I'll change my politics completely," he said. "Just to make you happy, I'll vote whatever way you want from now on. I'll do anything you think necessary." I was only still listening out of politeness. My mind was made up. I just wanted to get out of there as quickly as possible and never look back.

"You've built this big wall between us," I told him, thinking to finish matters on a philosophic note. "You'll just have to live on your side of it now, and I on mine." I slammed the door on my way out, and did a big screechy wheel spin pulling out of the driveway. It just seemed appropriate in the moment.

Running

for Helen Mort

The doctor told him he must do something about his weight, so my husband joined a running club for obese people. Soon he was clocking up kilometres three times a week and the pounds were disappearing steadily. Within six months he was looking better than ever and had to invest in a whole new wardrobe.

Most of the original group, by this point, had dropped out and gone back to eating pizzas and whole Swiss Rolls, and experiencing the odd cardiac event. It was just my husband and another woman left. He said they were training for a marathon.

Then one evening he went out for a run but didn't bother to come home. Six months have passed now and there's still no sign of him. Maybe they are running still, like in *Forrest Gump*, and maybe not. When friends ask after him, all I can do is shrug and tell them he's run off with another woman.

Rolo

I've always had something of an addiction to Nestlé Rolos, and I've done well enough out of offering my last one to a few girls down through the years.

On the last occasion, she and I were sitting on a park bench, enjoying the pack of sweets together beneath mild April sunshine.

"Go ahead, I want you to have it," I told her when only one sweet remained.

"Oh wow, total déjà vu," she said, and gobbled it up greedily.

"Is it?" I asked.

"Yeah. On Tuesday, remember? We were sitting here on this same bench and you said the same thing. It was you, wasn't it?"

"No, not me," I answered.

"Oh," she said, and it was really quiet and awkward for a while until she remembered there was this really important thing she had to go do.

Letters

My girlfriend thought it would be fun to each come up with three celebrity crushes that we would have one another's permission to sleep with if the opportunity ever presented itself. It never would, of course, so I agreed. It would be harmless fun. I fetched a bottle of wine while she got stationery.

"Who've you got?" she asked, seeing me scribbling a name.

"Jessica Alba," I answered.

"Seriously?" she hissed. "What's she got that I don't have?" She seemed very annoyed, but then she burst out laughing and said if I ever managed to get with Jessica Alba would I mind letting her join in. She's such a joker like that.

We had so much fun we wound up opening a second bottle of wine and getting really giddy. It had been a great way to pass an evening. The following day, however, she was at the desk in the study looking very business-like. I asked her what she was doing and she told me she was writing letters.

"To anyone important?" I asked.

"Oh yes," she said. "This one's to Matt Damon. Next, I'll write one to Dwayne Johnson, and then, last but not least, to Channing Tatum."

She became quite obsessed with writing letters to these three men, the ones from her list. Every few days she was writing more. Sometimes she'd even read them aloud to get my opinion, which is how I knew she was propositioning them in no uncertain terms.

She didn't seem to see any problem with any of this. She'd just ask if I thought she was coming on too strong, or if I thought she was coming across as desperate.

I really don't know what to do. I already tried talking to her about it. She was writing a letter at the time and said it was very hard to concentrate with me yapping away. "Would you mind going into town to pick up some more stationery?" she asked, an obvious ploy just to get me out of her hair for a while.

3

"I'm a ridiculously good-looking man now, so you can only imagine what I looked like in my twenties. Women fell over themselves to get to me. And I was generous enough to let them approach. But Emily caught wind of my extra-marital shenanigans, threatening to call the parish priest in, as if that was something that would concern me."

John Boyne
from *The Heart's Invisible Furies*

Cancer

My father-in-law insisted I leave. He said I was a complete disgrace, although technically he wasn't my father-in-law any longer, not since my beautiful wife lost her valiant battle with the cancer.

"You didn't hear her last words," I protested to him. "She told me not to waste any time grieving, and that life was just too short for sadness, and that I should move on and find happiness without delay." I could see it was useless, however. He wasn't getting it.

When I tried to kiss his other daughter, I was honouring my wife's dying wishes. Hers was the only other face in this world that could compare in beauty to my wife's, since they were identical twins, but I had a feeling he wasn't going to see it from my point of view, no matter how logically I explained it.

To save him from making an even bigger scene than he already had, I decided it was best to go. I kissed my wife's cold lips one last time and then left. I figured the last thing she'd want on the day of her funeral was for the two of us to be arguing over her.

Double

We couldn't really be mad at each other, because you need wrong and wronged. We were equally caught red-handed.

"I can explain this," my husband said, getting up from his chair. He stalled, his mouth hanging open. "Actually, I can't. It's exactly what it looks like." At that he sank dejectedly back into his seat.

In a moment of rotten luck, we'd chosen the same restaurant for our respective dates with non-spouses. I suppose we'd both heard all the great things that were being said about the food there. If that wasn't bad enough, we'd also had the misfortune of being seated at tables next to one another.

I looked at my husband's date, hoping she'd be fat but, to my great disappointment, she was a stunner. Before the waiter had even the time to put bread on the table, she came over and suggested we pull the tables together, make it a double date. You could see she was revelling in how bizarre the situation was.

"This is nice," I forced myself to say, ending a long, tense silence. It got easier, though. The wine helped, naturally, and by the third bottle we were all having a grand time, laughing loudly, disturbing other tables most likely.

The dates we'd brought were getting on famously, so well, in fact, that they fed each other their desserts and then left together, his hand caressing her perfect backside.

Taste

I seemed to be having a sudden sexual orientation crisis. I was catching myself gazing at handsome men in the street and, not only that, picturing them naked as well. I figured it was a little late for latency but I didn't know how else to explain the sordid fantasies in my mind, scenes taking place in hot tubs, on top of barroom pool tables, in bathroom cubicles and, of course, on remote tropical islands.

It all came very much out of the blue so you can imagine my alarm. I'd always felt so secure in my sexuality. I didn't know how or what to tell my darling wife but thought I'd better just be up front about it. That way, I hoped, we could deal with it together.

"I've been having sexual thoughts about other men," I told her. Luckily, she's a very empathetic woman, which is a quality I've always admired greatly in her.

"That's okay, dear, don't worry," she said. "I've been doing that for years." I breathed a huge sigh of relief and threw my arms around her. "This could actually be a good thing," she went on. "We might even have the same taste in men."

Elevator

for Samantha Foucault

My boyfriend and I were on an elevator with another couple, who we didn't know, when the power went out all of a sudden. We were stuck there in the darkness waiting either to be rescued or for the power to return.

After some initial cursing and groaning, we'd accepted our bad luck and begun settling down. After that, presumably out of awkwardness, nobody was saying anything, and the only sounds were our breathing and the occasional whinge of the cables holding us suspended. Thankfully everyone was calm and understood that we might as well get comfortable, so we all slid to the floor and sat there passing the time.

After a while we were finding ourselves more and more relaxed. Although there was still no conversation, we were actually becoming quite cosy and close together. It was as if there was an unspoken agreement that this was the best available means to pass the time, and so soon enough we were all kissing. I could hear the smooching sounds of the other couple as well, which was a relief because otherwise we might have felt bad about it.

There wasn't any tension because we were all on the same page. Kissing, as it tends to, gave way to explorative hands. The temperature had gone up very noticeably.

Then, without warning, the bright lights of the elevator flickered back on with retina-searing suddenness. I got the fright of my life when I realised what was happening. Somehow in the darkness we had become unwitting swingers. I was straddling a man I didn't know. My tongue had been in his mouth, his in mine. I looked across at my boyfriend and his hand was well and truly up the other girl's top. In fairness, he looked every bit as alarmed as I was feeling. I looked down and his zipper was undone and her hand had disappeared inside.

Mercifully, the elevator had restarted and was finishing its task of taking us to the ground floor. Still nobody managed to say anything as we composed ourselves, getting our trousers and tops and such back to a respectable state. There just wasn't anything to say at that point that might have made those few moments more bearable. There was nothing to be done other than go our separate ways and, maybe later, hope to see the funny side of it.

Desire

The oddest thing happened. I was in the midst of relations with my young, hard-bodied lover when all of a sudden I began thinking of my old, sagging husband. For years I've been suffering the most awful, hopeless sex with him, usually when he has come home drunk and insistent, and during those times I would close my eyes and think of others as best I could.

I've no idea how he came to intrude on my mind, or what it meant, and he was still old and hideous – not even the best version of himself, the one I married. I could even smell the comingling whiskey and urine stench that accompany him. My eyes were closed but my mind's eyes were wide open and gazing with longing into his incredibly ugly face. I'm just hoping it turns out to be a one-time thing, a dreadful glitch in my desire. God, I really hope it doesn't mean I fancy him. If it turns out I fancy him – I'm not even joking – I think I'll probably have to take my own life.

Goal

Knowing I'd be overjoyed, my girlfriend booked tickets for us to see Barcelona and Real Madrid at the Camp Nou.

"You really are the best," I said, beaming with excitement at the thought of at last seeing Messi and Suarez and Iniesta and all the rest.

To the match she wore the jersey I got for her, with Messi on the back of it. The atmosphere was getting inside her, I could tell. Soon she was cheering and singing and shouting out expletives at Ronaldo, Ramos and the referee. She was jumping up and down in the stands like a true Catalan, a genuine *Blaugrana*.

She got so caught up in it, when Messi scored a goal she grabbed another man and began ardently kissing him. He was very handsome, to be fair. I stood there watching them, four busy hands introducing themselves to new bodies. I didn't know how to react.

When the ref blew the final whistle they were still kissing.

"I'll see you back at the hotel?" I asked awkwardly, but there was no response, no evidence she'd even heard me. The stadium emptied and the floodlights went out and they continued kissing as though they had nothing else they wanted to do with the rest of their lives.

Fright

I took my fiancée to a theme park haunted house. I thought I'd take her there to call off the wedding and finish the relationship by introducing her to the new girl I'd been seeing, who was working for the park as a zombified cheerleader. She was nervous going in but I gripped her hand tightly, told her to be brave and that it would be over in no time.

"I don't know how else to say this, but it hasn't been working for a while," I explained to her after we'd come unscathed through the first few spooks. "Lately you just haven't seemed too bothered about us anymore, and I'm afraid I've met someone else." Just then, my new girlfriend appeared in a doorway. She began shambling towards us, face and clothes stained red with blood. She was waving pom poms in her hands and groaning very convincingly.

My poor fiancée didn't take the news well at all. She just began screaming in horror at the thought of losing me, which I hadn't expected at all. I really thought she'd take it in her stride. As I watched her shaking violently with dread, I was suddenly sure I was making a terrible mistake. I'd been a fool to ever have doubted the strength of her love. As she passed out with the fright, I could hardly wait for her to regain consciousness so I could take it all back.

Chips

I'd lost the girls after the nightclub, and had spent all my money on booze. I wasn't sure how I was getting home. That's when I saw him, sitting on a wall, munching away. I got the waft of his bag of chips and instantly had a massive craving.

"Any chance of a chip?" I called out.

"I'll give you a chip for a kiss," he answered, smiling drunkenly.

"Ah go on, don't be mean," I said.

"That's my offer," he said, and took a chip out of the bag and held one end of it between his teeth, pointing at the other end with a finger. I sat next to him and took the other end of it between my teeth. Our lips joined in a salt and vinegar kiss. The chip was delicious, crispy on the outside, floury on the inside.

"Can I use your phone?" I asked. "Mine's dead and I need to call my boyfriend to come collect me."

"What's the hurry?" he answered. "Here, have another chip."

Birthday

"Your birthday's coming up soon," my wife said. "Have you given any thought to what you might like?"

I told her I hadn't and then she got a grin on her face, the grin she always gets when she has a great idea and wants me to ask what her great idea is, and so I asked.

"I thought I might give you a very special present this year," she began. "I thought I might get you a woman for a one night only thing. Does that sound like fun or what?"

"Do you mean cheat on you?" I asked

"Oh don't think of it as cheating. Just think of it as a birthday present."

I was just thinking it must be a trap when she apparently read my mind, which she often seems to do.

"Don't worry, this isn't a trap," she assured me.

"And you'd be okay with this?" I asked, still not at all at ease.

"Of course I would. I just want to give you a very special present on your birthday. I promise there'll be no blame or guilt or jealousy, none of that stuff. In fact, I was hoping you might return the favour when my birthday comes around. There's this very nice new intern at work I have my eye on."

Return

My girlfriend was tired of having an affair and decided to leave me. I got boxes and sturdy black sacks and helped her pack her things, filling up the rented van, my back aching by the end of it. I had the absurd notion she might change her mind; that she might tell me to bring it all back in, she was staying.

"You were just too nice," she said, pinching my cheek, and then she was gone. I stood there coughing in the cloud of smoke from the van's exhaust, still waving her off as it put distance between us.

I kept her in my life as best I could, but it wasn't easy. I texted her to say I'd found a hair straightener beneath the couch and would return it. She said to keep it but I brought it anyway to the café where she works, knowing all too well how she hates it when her hair isn't straight.

The following week I found a Sylvia Day novel at the back of a cabinet, a bookmark between pages 94 and 95, and so I rushed it right over, very worried that she might buy a new copy before I arrived.

When weeks later I handed her a pair of hedge clippers over the counter, she told me that all of this really had to stop. She said I needed to move on, which meant no more excuses to come in and see her.

Finally, I brought Daisy, handing her across the counter in front of all her customers.

"But Daisy is your dog," she said, looking puzzled.

"I keep offering to take her for long walks and trying to feed her things she loves but she shows no interest," I explained, "and when I asked if she'd like to go live with her bitch of a mother, she started jumping around and wagging her tail and drooling. I think she must agree with you that I'm too bloody nice."

Swim

Having been brought up in the traditional way, I wanted nothing more than to find a wife who would stay at home, who would prepare dinner and raise children while I had a career. I got very lucky – after very little searching, I found a woman who told me that all she's ever wanted was to never have to work for a living. I knew she was the one.

She kept asking for money each day, and often very obscene amounts of it, and I would always hand it over without question, and I would feel like a real man for being able to do so. Such was my upbringing.

However, one day I got home from work and she told me she had to leave at once; that she had fallen in love and had no choice but to abandon our loveless, albeit convenient marriage. I told her it was not loveless at all – that I loved her very much – but she just pointed at the TV and said she saw the man she is meant to be with on the screen earlier and she has to go find him immediately, not resting until he is in her arms. She said she'd have left a note and been gone already only for needing money for flights and hotels and food.

"Lots of money," she said, "because this could take a while and I don't want to be out on the street." I said no, of course, feeling a little emasculated doing so for the first time but, of course, it wasn't because I didn't have it to give. I told her she was being silly, and to go to bed, and that she'd have forgotten about all this nonsense by the morning, at which time I'd accept a very mortified apology from her.

"Fine, have it your way so," she said. "I suppose I'll just have to swim across the ocean then, won't I?" Naturally, I thought she was bluffing, but then she actually got in the water and started swimming out after I mockingly drove her as far as the water's edge.

The rescue team brought her drowned body ashore and I identified her as my wife. When the authorities present asked what she was doing swimming out that far, I informed them quite matter-of-factly that she was crossing the ocean in search of the love of her life. They looked at me in shock for a long moment before telling me that this was hardly any time for making jokes.

"Who's joking?" I answered, but they continued to look at me with their gobs open. They just kept looking at me as though I'd said something only the very worst kind of person would ever say.

Cliff

My friend was inconsolable when she learned her husband was having a relationship with another woman, and apparently saw no alternative to throwing herself from a cliff onto the rocks below. An empty bottle of gin and an empty box of *Kleenex* were found in her abandoned car by the cliffside.

"Don't ever let it happen to you," she warned me the very last time we spoke.

I decided I'd better do what I could to heed her advice, so told my husband the full story of the betrayal she had suffered. I asked him as nicely as I could to never do that to me, just in case I might take it as badly as her.

I could tell he understood my concerns. The way he looked in my eyes let me know there was no cause for worry. When he assured me it would never, ever happen again, I could feel his sincerity down to my bones.

4

"You have to be clever to have a successful secret affair; you have to be ahead of the game, to plan and anticipate every little thing. Deceit uses up a lot of your energy."

Jackie Kay
from 'Married Women' in
Why Don't You Stop Talking

Standards

for Ellen Earls

I used to be very successful at being unfaithful, before the unfortunate accident at work. I was left severely disfigured and my life changed completely as a result. I wasn't anywhere near as handsome, for starters, but all I wanted was to continue being myself as best I could. I was very grateful for my incredible wife vowing to stand by me, though I would have understood if she felt she had to take the shallow option. Given the circumstances, I dropped my standards for a while but only found that even the plainest women thought they were too good for me. Being unfaithful was proving quite tricky, so I naturally became much better at staying true to my wife. In fact, since I was being turned down by such unspectacular women, I thought I'd do my self-esteem some good. Now I have the highest standards of rejection. I insist on being turned down by only the very best looking women. I don't waste my time with anything less. Sometimes I see minor beauties looking horrified by my melted face and must assure them that I have no intentions of hitting on them. I assure them that they can relax. They usually seem very insulted but I can't help that. It's not my fault they're not pretty enough.

Turtles

for Susan Millar DuMars

I was distraught when she finally told me the truth. All our years together, all I'd ever done was worship her as best I could, and wished for nothing more than to spend the rest of my days trying to improve on it.

"I thought it was just meaningless sex for a while," she explained, "a bit of fun, nothing more, but things have changed. We've decided we owe it to ourselves to have a real go at a future together."

"But what about the great future we talked about?" I asked.

"Please, there's no need for a big scene," she said, looking around her to see if anyone was taking notice. "That's why I took you to the supermarket at peak time to tell you this. Show a bit of consideration for the staff and other shoppers. I'm sure they don't need to see you falling apart."

"What about Lennon and McCartney?" I asked, meaning our two turtles. I was doing my best to stay calm and composed, holding back the tears that were trying to fall. "Shouldn't we stay together for their sakes?" I knew I was grasping at straws.

"No," she said, "we really shouldn't. I will be taking full custody of them, naturally, since you probably won't take all of this in your stride, and will surely become quite depressed, possibly even suicidal. If you care about their happiness, and I believe you do, I'm sure you'll agree that this is really in their best interests."

Drawing

When my girlfriend said she and a few of the girls were going to a life drawing class, which guaranteed she'd be out of the apartment every Thursday evening, I felt like I'd hit the jackpot.

"Of course I'd invite you to join us," she said, "but the class is only for women."

"Thank you, dear," I said. "It sounds like a lot of fun." I was really just thinking about all the extra video game time I'd be gaining.

Several months into it, it occurred to me to go through her sketchpad for the first time. She had never shown me anything she had drawn during the classes, I was suddenly aware, but I figured maybe I'd just not shown the interest. I was horrified to see that they were all of men, all with gym memberships, and all very generously proportioned you know where. It was hardly any wonder these people were all so eager to be drawn in the nip by a bunch of women.

I knew I hadn't any genuine right to feel betrayed by her. She'd told me where she was, what she was doing. If I didn't know any more detail, it was because I'd not asked the questions.

My imagination started getting the better of me, creating the sort of conversations they might have had together afterwards in the pub, and they weren't anything to do with drawing. It was nothing but talk about the gorgeousness of the male model and the abundance of his member. Shrill, dirty laughter filled my mind when someone would say something very rude about what she'd like to do to him. Sometimes, it was my girlfriend who made the remarks that brought about the cackles.

I should mention that her drawing has improved drastically over the time she has been going. Despite my great shock, I was also very impressed. At this rate she might soon be quite renowned for drawing handsome, well-endowed nude men standing by a window looking out at whatever's there.

Truly

The naivety of marriage is really a very beautiful thing — the joyful innocence, the optimism, all the hope of it. I mean that with no cynicism. Like it was only yesterday, I remember standing on that altar and looking at you, the man of my dreams, and speaking those vows, and saying "I do" and then kissing you and heading out of the church amid chiming bells into our wonderful, perfect future. I really meant every word of those promises I made. I can't say that with quite enough seriousness. I think it's so important that you know that. I accept you may have your doubts, and not without reason. Though I didn't quite keep them, please, do try to see that it doesn't necessarily change the fact that I truly, truly meant them, one hundred per cent, when I spoke them. I was very, very sure we were forever. I realise it's probably hard to believe that now, but I swear it. Though it has only been two weeks and we find ourselves getting divorced because I've had difficulties with regard to not sleeping with other men, it really would pain me greatly if you were to believe I was anything less than deadly serious in all I said that day. I honestly had no idea there would so many extraordinarily handsome men on that island you picked out for our honeymoon.

Bravo

It was very exciting to discover that my new girlfriend was an actress. On seeing my great interest in what she does for a living, she invited me to attend a rehearsal for her new play. She was playing the lead female role in a new romantic tragedy.

I went along and sat there proudly with a goofy smile on my face as they played out various scenes, and I have to say, I was very impressed with what I was seeing. I imagined it was going to be a fine production that would receive rave reviews from the critics.

Then the director called for places for the big kiss scene, and she and a very handsome actor met in the centre of the stage. Soon they were kissing each other very passionately and as though they were very much in love. I sat there uneasily and told myself that they were acting, nothing more.

They rehearsed the scene several times and each time they seemed to kiss more passionately than the time before. The director was so impressed by their progress that he ordered more and more takes. I was not enjoying myself at all anymore.

My girlfriend and the man left the theatre then. His arm was around her still. She held his hand against her chest, and they walked out into the light of day. Was this part of the play, I wondered. I followed them out, keeping at a distance, not entirely sure and not wanting, if it was, to break their concentration. Then she inserted her other hand inside the arse pocket of his tight jeans.

Eventually they came to a house and went inside. This can't be a part of the rehearsal still, can it, I wondered. The director and the other crew and actors were nowhere to be seen, I couldn't help noticing. I stood outside the house waiting, but for what, I didn't know. After a while I became impatient and went to a window. They were there on the couch, naked and making love.

If this was still acting, they really were giving the performance of a lifetime, even though it was only a rehearsal. I thought about applauding rapturously, but I realised I should really wait until they were finished, just in case, and so I waited, and waited, and waited. By then several hours had passed. I must say, they seemed to get quite a fright when I finally let out my shouts of Bravo! Bravo! Bravo!

Volume

After more conventional efforts failed, I thought bringing other men home for sex in our bed might provoke a response out of my husband. Since he lost his job, he's just been moping around in sweatpants and stained t-shirts, spending most of the time on the couch watching *Netflix* and devouring family packs of salt and vinegar crisps. It just breaks my heart to see him living like this.

I keep hoping he'll come charging up the stairs, kick in the door and become the man I married again, so each time I try to make even more noise than the last. It has become very loud but, unfortunately, without any success yet. He just turns up the volume on his new surround sound, and occasionally prods at the ceiling with a broomstick he keeps within reach. I refuse to give up on him, though. This can't all be for nothing. I have to keep trying, keep believing the next man I bring home is the one.

Photos

My fiancée poured two glasses of a shiraz that had been recommended to us, telling me she had some photos she was excited to show me. As she turned the pages of the album, taking sips of the wine in between, she said a little bit about each one, such as when and where it was taken. I have to admit, it was a little disconcerting when each new photo revealed her pretty, smiling face, with one handsome man after another stood next to her.

"Who are all these men, dear?" I asked, doing my best to seem unconcerned. I'm fairly sure she noticed my concern, judging by the way she touched my hand reassuringly with hers.

"Old boyfriends," she replied. "These are all the men I knew before I met you – before I met the love of my life."

Naturally, I breathed a sigh of relief. Then I suddenly felt quite good about myself, the realisation sinking in that she'd chosen me above all these men, all of whom could easily have modelling careers.

"Do you still think of any of them?" I asked. I can't say why I asked it but I did, regretting it immediately.

"Oh yes, quite regularly, in fact," she answered, still stroking my hand lovingly. "Especially this one," she went on, her finger tapping the picture of the most handsome of the lot.

Chess

"I've met someone else," he said, "but there's no need to despair just yet. I'll give you one more chance to prove that you're the one." He was setting up a chessboard as he spoke.

"Okay. What must I do to prove it?" she asked.

"You win," he explained, "and I'll tell her it's over and I'll never see her again. I win, and you immediately pack your bags and leave and don't ever come back."

"Okay," she said again, trying her utmost to appear grateful for the chance. "I've never played chess before."

"I know," he replied, "but I know the game very well. Don't worry, I will explain it all as we go along."

Faithful

I am married to a good and giving man and really do know my luck to say it so surely. For what he lacks in style and charisma, he makes up for in consistency and security.

I have been attempting to have an affair, though. I felt a need for some excitement, something illicit, and so began going into bars by myself to seduce lonely drinkers. I propositioned many but there haven't been any takers so far. There was even one in particular who, sitting at the counter in a hotel bar, turned around on his stool and, looking at me, vomited into cupped hands, dropping their contents then in a loud splash onto the tiles before running out the door, a near-full pint of beer left behind him.

So yes, I am a faithful wife, for the time being at least, and strictly speaking. I'm not giving up, however. I won't be deterred by this evidence that I'm less than a beauty queen. He is out there. I'm so sure he is out there, my man of danger, my man of excitement, my man of very low standards.

Rockstar

My friends are all very envious that I have a famous rockstar girlfriend. They have very ordinary girlfriends – teachers and nurses and secretaries – while my girlfriend makes albums and plays concerts all around the world.

"How did you ever get a woman like that to go out with you?" they ask. I never take any offense to it because I have no idea. I just enjoy it and all its benefits.

She told me at the beginning of our relationship that she doesn't ever want to have a famous boyfriend.

"Oh, don't worry," I said, "I have no talents at all, so I'm your ideal man," and she laughed and I laughed along with her. It was actually pure luck that the sad truth came out charmingly.

Sometimes friends ask me if I worry about what she might be getting up to when away on tour. Funnily enough, I don't. I trust her completely. Ironically, it's me that's up to no good when she's on tour. It's amazing how having a rockstar girlfriend makes you so desirable to women who'd never otherwise look twice at you. I guess they all can't help wondering what she sees in me either, and there's only one way to find out.

Hurt

My husband came clean about having slept with another woman. He described her as a masochist, whatever that is. He said he was not giving up on our marriage, however.

"I just need more from you," he said. "I really do think we have a future still."

"What do you need from me?" I asked. Despite the pain, I loved him and would do anything to make it work.

"It's the sex," he said. "It's just a bit safe, a bit boring. If it could be less safe and boring, I know we can make it work."

I couldn't believe he could be so cruel, so hurtful. I lost control, anger taking me over, and ran at him, kicking him in the balls and dropping him heavily to the floor. Immediately I regretted it, felt awful for it. "I'm sorry," I blurted out. "I don't know what came over me."

"No," he said, writhing around, holding himself, "don't be sorry. That's exactly what I'm talking about. That feels amazing. I need more of that."

Yarn

Jason, our cat, knows the truth, so I feed him some tuna and stroke his sleek black fur and tell him he's a very good kitty.

"That will be our little secret, Jason," I say once more, but like it's the first time.

"Meow," he answers, rubbing himself up against my bare legs, thanking me, his belly full now. He always accepts the bribe.

Later, my husband will get in from work. No doubt it will have been another very tough day. That's what he always says, falling in a depressing heap onto the couch.

I will look conspiratorially at Jason, smile at his inscrutable little cat face, once again giving away nothing of what's happened here earlier. Just like last time, then, I'll roll a ball of yarn across the linoleum for him to chase. It's just an understanding we have.

5

"Again she flew at him, pushing her breasts into his body and kissing his closed lips. 'I love you, Perico. I love you. Everyone knows Consuela's fat and ugly. They laugh at her. Make love to me. I'll be your mistress if I can't be your wife.'"

Dan Rhodes
from 'Beautiful Consuela' in
Don't Tell Me the Truth About Love

Bisexual

One afternoon, as we were sat enjoying some silence and a glass of chardonnay, my wife mentioned having suspicions that she might be a bisexual.

"I've been looking at other women and thinking things," she confessed. "Lewd sorts of things."

"I see," I answered. It was all I could manage to say at first, feeling taken aback, but I always pride myself on being an understanding and supportive husband, so eventually suggested that she go out and sleep with three women.

"That should help you to know for sure," I said, and laid my hand tenderly on hers.

"Is there no end to your understanding?" she asked, leaning in, kissing my cheek.

We went to bars together and I helped her strike up conversations with loose-looking women drinking alone, then I'd leave discreetly and go home to watch boxsets and await her key in the latch. Three women later, she sat me down and told me that she is, without a doubt, not a bisexual.

"That's absolutely wonderful," I said, "we can go back to normal now."

"I'm actually a lesbian," she said.

"Oh," I said.

"I'm very sorry," she said. "Really I am. You deserve the very best."

"I think there is a part of me that always knew," I admitted.

"Yes," she said, nodding in agreement. "I guess I must have pulled some strange faces at the sight of it. That thing never did look quite right to me."

Limp

I developed a big crush on my brother's fiancée. I didn't mean to. She was beautiful, of course, but so much more. It was one of those things that just sort of happened. Before too long, I was finding myself distracted very often, and getting lost in quite vivid, sexual daydreams of her. I'd never had these thoughts about another woman until I met her but, once I had, men seemed to lose all their appeal for me.

I debated over and over again with myself whether or not to tell her my feelings, as well as whether or not to confess them to my brother. The last thing I wanted to do was hurt him. Unfortunately, I ended up waiting until the wedding ceremony to tell both of them, as well as the priest and all their guests. It was the last opportunity, it dawned on me, when I heard the priest deliver that line, "speak now or forever hold your peace."

"Stop," I shouted, and began running up the aisle to intervene. I knew I shouldn't have worn such high heels. I fell over and landed quite awkwardly on one hip. I had to drag myself up and then limp the rest of the way to the altar. Everyone was waiting for me. Time was passing and I could feel the tension building, everyone present eager to know the reason for my objection.

I told them both that they were making a big mistake, and that they couldn't possibly be meant to be together. I grabbed her hand then, preparing for the run out of the church together that you see in all the films, the sham marriage prevented. However, when I tried to move, there was a strong pull in my arm that prevented me. I turned around to see the look of sheer horror on their faces, knowing then she didn't feel the same way.

I limped back to my seat through the most dreadful silence. When I got there, my husband couldn't even look at me. His head was bowed and shaking from side to side, the way it does when he's absolutely mortified.

Cheat

I was playing *Monopoly* with the family because it was 'family night'. Every Wednesday evening we would spend some quality time together, all five of us – board games, movies, charades and such. I was trying, as always, to gain an unfair advantage. The children, though, hawk-eyed, were watching my every move, counting places out as I moved my marker.

"Daddy's a cheat!" David called out, laughing as he did so, and Becky and Shaun joined in the hysterics. Playing along with the fun, I turned to my wife for defence but there was only the knowing look in her weepy eyes.

Personality

for Dan Rhodes

My wife has a great personality, maybe even the best personality. She really has. Honest to God, I sometimes find myself in complete awe of it. She's the most fascinating conversationalist, and she also has a knack for saying the sweetest, most thoughtful things at exactly the right moments.

I use the internet to find and meet women without personalities – lots of beautiful, shallow women with excellent boobs and sculpted backsides; women who have never really needed personalities, and so never bothered to develop any. Now and again I've asked some of them if they ever considered developing one but each of them just scoffed, as if the idea was completely ludicrous.

Guys

I've noticed that my girlfriend has far too many guy friends. It really concerns me. There just doesn't seem to be any girls she hangs out with.

"I get on better with guys," she tells me, shrugging, when I suggest the possibility of making a few female friends.

The other thing that really concerns me is how flirtatious she gets with her friends, even right in front of me. Sometimes it feels like I don't even exist to her.

"Is it that time of the month again?" she jokes, whenever I try to explain to her how it makes me feel.

I do my best to convince myself it's my own insecurity that's the problem. I tell myself over and over that I need to work on my own self-esteem and that if I do that I won't even notice these silly little issues anymore.

"I'm sorry I get so clingy sometimes," I told her just the other day. "I'm working on it." I was setting out some snacks at the time because a bunch of guys she knows were on the way over for drinks and video games.

"That's okay," she said, giving me a playful slap on the bottom. "It's actually kind of sweet when you get all worried and hormonal."

Scotch

If Moses were around today, I'm sure even he wouldn't be so uptight about a little adultery. I don't think it would make his list. The times change, after all, and everybody has to get with them. I was happy enough to turn a blind eye to my wife fooling around behind my back. I'm not a hypocrite so saw no point in turning it into a big deal. I've even been decent enough to carry on like she's been doing a good job of covering her tracks when, in all honesty, she's been fairly sloppy.

There has to be somewhere the line is drawn, though. I've just been to the liquor cabinet and near half the very rare, very expensive bottle of scotch I've been saving is gone. I know she doesn't ever touch the stuff, so she's obviously served it to his nibs. I mean, anyone with even a shred of respect would have tried topping it up again with an inferior scotch and hoped for the best. I've never been so angry in my all life. When she gets in there's going to be hell to pay. This is really unforgiveable.

Blue

My jeweller showed me the finest pair of blue sapphire earrings and immediately I said I'd take them.

"They're perfect," I told him and handed over my credit card. "My girlfriend has the most striking pair of blue eyes to match these." I was already thinking of my rewards and couldn't wait to surprise her.

"They're absolutely stunning," she said, putting them on and insisting we go out for a romantic meal so she can show them off.

"Don't you mean so I can show you off?" I flirted.

It was only when she was sitting across from me in the candlelight that I became aware of my terrible mistake.

I looked into her greenish eyes and realised it's my other girlfriend has the striking pair of blues. I felt very silly, naturally, but then figured it was no great harm done. I might have said something about how they bring out her beautiful blue eyes but, thankfully, I'd not put my foot in it this time.

Popcorn

My girlfriend had been unemployed for a long time and I'd been paying the bills as best I could. She'd say she doesn't want to do just any old thing, which I could appreciate, but the professions she was listing often required qualifications she just didn't have.

"You will have to go to university for that," I told her sympathetically when she asked my thoughts about her becoming a dermatologist. As much as I loved her, my patience endured considerable testing.

When she arrived home one day with the news that she'd been offered a job I was overjoyed. I threw my arms around her and whooped with excitement.

She's a professional escort now and the money is terrific. Our standard of living has more than doubled and we moved into a vastly superior apartment and can go on the most lavish of foreign holidays.

As time passes I'm getting more and more comfortable with what she does for a living. I was uneasy for a while, but I could never say anything because she just seemed so happy and fulfilled, and what kind of boyfriend would I be to deny her that?

Now I simply ask how her day went and she tells me the less I know the happier I'll be, and I say okay and continue making the popcorn while she picks out a movie to watch.

Who

My boyfriend announced that he was leaving me for another woman.

"So, who is she?" I asked, but he just waved the question away with his hand, said it hardly matters; that it was done and that's that. No 'I'm sorry', no explanation, no tears that might indicate I'd meant something to him these two years we'd spent – I had thought – so blissfully in love.

"We can work it out, I'm sure we can," I pleaded, and gripped his arm with two hands as he tried to turn away.

"I'm afraid not," he answered. "We can't work it out, but I really do hope you and your sister can."

League

I was dating a strikingly beautiful girl who I knew to be way out of my league. I'm not quite sure how it happened that she said yes to going out with me but, then again, you see that happening all the time. It's just something that happens to other people, never to you. Yet, here it was: my turn. I was determined not to overthink it, to just enjoy it.

I couldn't help myself, though. Insecure thoughts just kept popping into my mind each time I looked at her beautiful face or touched the exquisite contours of her gym-sculpted body. I'd try to swat them away but, like bees, they just kept coming straight back more insistently than before.

I eventually had to bring it up with her. I couldn't resist — I just had to know what it was she saw in me. She smiled appreciatively when I did, as though I might have saved her some awkwardness by bringing it up. She admitted to being aware that I wasn't exactly an oil painting, and that I perhaps didn't have much in the way of riches or brains or personality or talent, but she was quite adamant that I not sell myself short either.

"I'm seeing some other guy as well," she said with a big weary sigh, "and he's your quintessential handsome, stylish, charming guy, good at everything, and going places. He's pretty much perfect, so far as I can tell. I always feel so damn self-conscious around him, wondering if he might be about to realise I'm not pretty enough, or not smart enough. That's why I love being with you." She laid a soft hand on my pasty, pimply cheek and looked into my eyes to heighten the intimacy of the moment.

"You're very special to me like that," she continued. "When I'm with you, I never doubt myself, never question myself. It's like as if I'm bullet proof. Whatever it is about you, you never fail to make me feel like a million bucks."

Affair

My wife was coming home late nearly every night, always exhausted, and so naturally enough I suspected she was having an affair. I decided I'd better start having a few of my own, not to be letting her have all the fun. It wasn't easy at all. I kept asking people in the supermarket, the dry cleaners, coffee shops, all kinds of places, if they'd be interested, but they weren't. People are not as excited about having affairs as Hollywood films would have you believe they are.

Eventually, though, there was one who was interested. I'll admit, interested is maybe overstating it, but she agreed to do it. It was a huge relief. She really wasn't much to look at, if I'm being honest, but I'd run out of options. It was her or no one.

It turned out then my wife had not been having an affair at all. Rather, she had gotten a second job, and was going from one to the other in the evening. She didn't tell me because she felt I might talk her out of it due to concern for her wellbeing. When she had enough money saved up she gave me the news that we were going to the World Cup. The excitement I felt rushing through me was indescribable. It's what I've always wanted. Of course, I feel so ridiculous for having doubted her. Naturally, I immediately called off the affair.

Us

My wife confessed to being unfaithful, but she wanted to be very clear that she was not giving up on us. She wanted to assure me she'd never felt so ashamed of herself and was going to do everything she could to make things right. I could see she was distraught and so took her in my arms and rubbed her back in a very soothing way and told her not to worry.

"Then you can forgive me?" she asked, hope in her voice.

"Now, now, there's nothing to forgive," I replied softly, dabbing her weeping eyes with a tissue. "I've been unfaithful many, many times. I probably should've mentioned this sooner, but I gave up on us ages ago."

6

"If you are having an affair, it could save your relationship. If you are not having an affair, and your relationship is rocky, then perhaps you should."

Chloe Thurlow
from *Katie in Love*

Wedding

I'd put it off long enough and it just wasn't fair on anyone concerned, so I bit the bullet and told my fiancée that I must call off the wedding.

"I can't marry you," I said. "I've met someone else, you see, and I didn't plan for this to happen, but we're falling in love and I'm sure that it's her I'm meant to be with."

She said she wasn't about to give up without a fight and, sure enough, that evening an email came through from her. She'd clearly gone out that afternoon and bought an array of the skimpiest and sexiest lingerie she could find, and had then taken a bunch of photos of herself in them and striking various provocative poses. In each one she was making very flirtatious faces or blowing kisses at the camera.

Then a text message came through:

"Are you sure you want to kiss all of this goodbye?" it read, and there was a little puckered red lips emoji at the end. I had to hand it to her. I believe in giving credit where it's due and, no exaggeration, these photos could probably convert homosexuals, and yet I wasn't persuaded, and still had to insist on calling off the wedding.

"I see," she said in a defeated tone. "So then there's definitely no way I can change your mind?"

"No," I said sorrowfully.

"So I guess she's just incredibly beautiful and sexy and I just can't compete, is that it?" she asked.

"Well, actually," I answered, "in conventional terms, I'd have to say that you are much prettier and sexier than she is, there's just something there that I can't begin to explain to myself, never mind to anyone else. It's like as if it's a spell I've been put under."

"Do you have a picture of her you could show me?" she asked.

"I do," I said, taking out my phone and logging onto *Facebook*. I showed her my new girlfriend's profile picture, which is a very good photo of her, I believe — a photo that shows her at her modest best.

"You're right," she said, scrutinizing the picture. "She really is very plain. I am vastly better looking than her, there's no doubt about it, and much sexier as well." She seemed suddenly quite pleased with herself and all of the defeated tone was well and truly gone out of her voice.

"I am sorry," I said. "I truly never meant for you to get hurt."

"Who said I'm hurt?" she asked, and a massive, exquisite smile appeared on her face, one fit for the happiest day of her life.

Fool

My wife has a great sense of humour. There's nothing more attractive, if you ask me. She played a very good joke on me only yesterday. I got in and there was a note on the kitchen table letting me know she'd been having a torrid love affair with my father, and it had been going since the day before our wedding.

"I understand this is quite distressing news," the note went on, "so I have left a loaded gun in your sock drawer so that, if you want to, you can take the easy way and never have to deal with any of this pain. Please, though, try not to make too much of a mess. And do it away from my favourite Persian rug."

Naturally, I went to check the sock drawer. There was no gun. Instead I found another note, a much briefer one. "Happy April Fools' Day," it read, in big letters, and she'd drawn a big smiley face beneath it.

She's always playing cute little practical jokes like that on me. Just when I think I can't possibly love her any more!

Harley

After two wonderful years together, my girlfriend told me she couldn't continue with the betrayal. I really was stunned. I was under the impression things were great between us and only going from strength to strength in every way.

"I'm sorry," she told me, "but you're just too damn nice. I need someone who knows how to be bad, who likes a bit of danger, and you're just not him." At least that's what I think she said. It wasn't so easy to be sure. After all, at the time she was sitting on the back of a Harley Davidson, gripping onto a large, leather-wrapped man, and it was quite difficult making out her exact words over the gunning of the engine.

Attention

My wife is always telling me that I don't pay any attention when she's talking to me. It isn't true at all, of course, since I can always repeat exactly what she was saying before the accusation is made. I suppose it's possible that sometimes it seems like I'm a million miles away, if I'm making eyes at another woman in the room, for instance, or texting another woman to arrange plans for later, but that doesn't mean for a second that the mundane details of my true love's day are not of the utmost importance to me. I can never get mad about it. When I repeat word for word what she was saying the poor thing just gets so embarrassed, clearly feeling awful, and I just have to hug her tightly, letting her know I'm not one bit upset with her.

Notches

I met a beautiful girl and we had been getting along very well for the two weeks we'd known each other before she finally invited me into her apartment. Each day I'd been more and more excited by the new relationship and realised we were about to take things to the next level.

After a few drinks it was all heating up. Our hands were suddenly pulling and tugging at each other's clothing. Then, still undressing one another, we were stumbling down the hall towards her bedroom.

"Before we go any further," she said, "there's something I have to warn you about." She sounded very serious, worried even.

"What is it?" I asked.

"You see, I care about you so much. I think we really could have a future," she said, "so I just don't want you to get the wrong idea about me."

"You can tell me anything," I responded. "I promise not to judge you."

"Okay. Well... I've loads of notches made on my bedposts," she confessed, "and I'm afraid they are exactly what they appear, but they're from a different life; they're from my life before I met you."

All night we made the most beautiful love and when I woke up the next morning I felt that everything was different; that the world had tilted onto some new, more favourable angle. I had fallen for her in a big way. I could feel it. When she turned over and looked at me, smiling, I was in even deeper again.

She kissed me and went to take a shower. I couldn't help myself. I counted the notches while she was gone. There was a staggering number. She was right to warn me. I'd really rather not say what the total was. A previous life, I reminded myself.

She came back in from the shower, smiling that smile again, wrapped in a big white towel, ringlets of wet hair around her shoulders.

"So then... When was the last time you put a notch in the bedpost?" I asked. I had to. I knew it would plague me if I didn't.

"Oh, just about twenty minutes ago," she said. "You were still asleep so I carved it quietly." She nodded towards a penknife on the locker.

"But what about what you said last night?" I asked. "About them being from a different life? About us having a future?"

"Oh, don't feel bad," she said, sitting down next to me on the edge of her bed and placing a soothing hand on my knee. "You didn't really think you were the only one for me, did you? That was just something I tell guys to preserve the romance, so they don't get a fright, you know? It works too. I can see you're a bit disappointed, but if it makes you feel any better, if I had any interest in being monogamous, although you might not be number one, I think you could have a fairly decent chance of making the top ten."

Golf

When my husband took up golf, I was certain golf was another woman, and I can't say I was too bothered about it. I just couldn't picture him playing golf, making that silly little stance you see them make on the TV, tapping the ball with his putter, while I could quite easily see him with another woman. I was sure he bought the set of golf clubs and all the gear for my benefit.

Isn't it ironic? Eighteen years the affair I had went on, each Sunday while he was supposedly playing golf – a year for each hole. I was so sure golf was another woman that I never needed to make sure.

One Sunday, then, he suffered a heart attack. I received a call from the manager at the golf club who broke the news gently. My husband had hit a glorious tee shot on the twelfth hole and then started clutching his chest. I went immediately to the hospital he'd been taken to but I was just too late.

"He's gone, I'm afraid," I was told by a nurse in the corridor. I went in and found him laid out, looking, I must say, very peaceful. He was wearing the most ridiculous outfit you ever saw, an outfit no one in their right mind would be seen dead in.

Explosion

She hadn't slept properly in days. Her late husband just kept turning up in her dreams. Mangled and bloodied, he kept pointing a melting, accusatory finger in her direction, though she wasn't guilty of the freak explosion that killed him.

Yes, she was having an affair, and yes, it would have made things less complicated if he could have just vanished out of existence, but that doesn't mean she'd ever have gone as far as planting a bomb under his car. Though hardly a perfect wife, she did love him in her own way.

Was this his ghostly vengeance she was experiencing? Or was it a simple manifestation of her terrible guilt? His funeral was only a week ago, and she'd put on quite the performance of dutiful, devoted wife. Guilt was a strong possibility.

There was, of course, also that one little joke she made once to her lover, about how much better things would be if somebody would just kill her husband. There'd be no more sneaking around, for starters, she pointed out, and then laughed giddily and shook her head at her own silliness. It was just a joke, though – a perfectly innocuous joke. There was no way he could possibly have taken it seriously.

Vows

I should have stuck with the traditional vows. If they were good enough for millions of people before me then there wasn't any reason why they shouldn't do just fine, but my fiancée had thought it a marvellous idea when I announced my intention to write my own unique words for the occasion.

Unfortunately, they turned out to be terribly negative and depressing. Even though they were honest and came from the heart, I could see soon after that they'd not been at all appropriate.

"Please, please, please, don't ever betray me," I pleaded on the altar, witnessed by both our families and all our friends, recorded by the videographer. It just isn't the most positive or celebratory message.

I don't know what I was thinking, going on for several minutes about how I'd been betrayed by many ex-girlfriends, and going into some rather specific detail about the great times they claimed to have while being unfaithful.

I've only myself to blame for what's happened. If the thought never entered her head before, no doubt my vows will have put it there.

It was very awkward that evening when I walked in on her with the best man. I just barged in without so much as a knock. I've never been so mortified. Naturally I told them I was very sorry for putting them in this position. I assured them as best I could that they were the victims here, and that I'd be accepting full responsibility for everything.

Machinery

A terrible machinery accident at work left my wife without her good looks. When the doctors finally unpeeled all the bandaging from her face, it was even worse than expected, and I'd been warned to expect the worst. It was as if she'd walked off the set of a horror film.

I'm trying to be supportive, of course, but the physical attraction is completely gone. How could it not be? I'm going to keep doing the best I can to continue loving her as much as I always have, but I don't imagine it'll be easy.

To give it its best shot at success, I've decided I must start having affairs with sexy, attractive women. I figure it's the only way to avoid becoming bitter about the loss of a healthy sex life with my wife. I'll be happy to hug her still, even to hold hands, and I'll try my best to look at her without thinking her hideous, but that will have to be as far as it goes.

Naturally, I'll take every precaution I can to prevent her finding out about these other women. She's been through enough, after all, and there's nothing I wouldn't do to protect her from further pain.

Comet

I agreed to marry a scientist. Bright and ambitious, I was sure he was going places, though he has never been the most romantic of men.

There was due to be a comet and I thought we might watch it together while enjoying some bubbly. He didn't seem all that enthusiastic but did at least agree.

"Isn't it beautiful?" I gasped. It was my first time seeing such a marvel.

"It's a fairly run of the mill Solar System body of ice and dust passing close to the sun," he replied with a shrug, seeming very bored.

I began dating a poet behind his back, thinking it the best solution. The backside of his trousers was wearing thin and he lived in total squalor, but he spoke so beautifully, so irresistibly. He created romance from the most ordinary things.

The first night we spent together we were dizzy on cheap cider when we came across a cat that had been run over. He knelt by the mess and spoke the most poignant, prayer-like words and I felt myself tingle at them. I was suddenly in a great hurry to be out of my clothes and feeling the weight of his starving body on mine.

Redemption

It's probably not unusual, someone in my condition asking to see the priest all the time. When you're young and healthy, sins just don't seem like a very big deal. You get used to treating absolution like an annoying form you can put in a drawer until later. Going to church and praying seem like a massive waste of time. Then you're much older and a doctor gives you some bad news and you think, what the hell did I do with that form?

They said it wouldn't take long and all of sudden I started having big concerns about the state of my soul. It's a bit like going to school and finding out you have an exam, then spending ten minutes cramming for it when all you had to do was to give a crap sooner and you'd have been fully prepared. Those ten minutes might be the difference between passing and failing, though – between Heaven and Hell.

I asked the priest if I should tell my wife I'd been unfaithful once, a very long time ago, and he said I must, and that way God would also know I really mean it when I repent. That terrible night made me a far better husband for all the years that followed, but unfortunately guilt is not redemption. That's what he told me when I tried to persuade him that maybe there was no need to tell her.

I did as he instructed. I told her my awful shame from all those years ago. She didn't take it very well, made it clear she would have left me all those years ago if she'd only known the truth. All our happy years were undone in an instant, and I was suddenly asking her forgiveness for ruining her whole life. She forgave neither. Instead, she took a pillow from under my head and began smothering me with it. It was hard to speak clearly at the time, so she may not have been able to make it out, but I told her that I love her very much and that I'd make it up to her, God willing, in the next life.

Costume

I came across a very nice girl on a packed dancefloor on Halloween night. She had an excessively slutty costume on but, to give her due credit, she had the body for it. I danced up behind her, putting my hands on her hips, and she shook her bottom against me. I was positive I was going to get lucky.

After dancing for a while longer in a very raunchy fashion, we finally took our masks off so we could kiss. I burst out laughing when I realised what had happened. It was my own girlfriend I'd been dancing with all along. She joined in and we spent the next several minutes in complete hysterics. I mean, there just didn't seem much point in getting upset about it.

7

"I reached the conclusion that there is a higher law than monogamy. A higher law than monogamy and fidelity. Sometimes it seems to me that the sin is not to be unfaithful, but to *not* be unfaithful."

Rob Doyle
from 'Barcelona' in
This is the Ritual

Treatment

My husband broke nearly every bone in his body during a terrible skiing accident. The doctors examined the results and determined that his was a very rare case where a full recovery just might be possible. They said he would need to work very hard in rehabilitation, and would need the best care to stand the best chance. We immediately contacted who they assured us was the best professional money could buy.

I must say, I thought it very bizarre when, first day on the job, she turned up in a mini-skirt, stilettos and a very skimpy top scarcely able to contain her full, luscious young breasts, which could quite easily have burst out at any moment.

Session after session she turned up dressed similarly. She arrived in leather, PVC, fishnet tights, you name it. I asked friends and they said they'd never heard the like. I'd catch him looking at her as she put him through various stretches and exercises. She would encourage him and then praise him. I'd see his eyes leering over her curves, travelling up and down the impossible lengths of her marvellous legs. She must have been aware of it, too, but never did anything to cover herself up. Unable to go on this way, I decided I'd just have to confront her about it.

"I'm so glad you asked," she told me. "It's a very important part of his treatment, you see." She smiled sweetly at me as though I should be reassured.

"I'm afraid you've lost me," I answered. "What do you mean it's a part of his treatment?"

"Oh, it's really quite simple," she went on. "It's all about effective motivation. Each day that your husband spends wanting nothing more than to have sex with me is yet another day he is pushing himself towards making a complete recovery." She flashed the sweet smile again. "Each day I must make him want it so bad that he is ignoring all the excruciating pain and hard work that this is taking. You must trust me when I say this is the best treatment he can get."

Destiny

I've got much more free time now since she left me for him. In order to not be sitting around in dark rooms imagining them having the wild, passionate, acrobatic sex they are presumably having, I took up a hobby to pass the time more pleasantly, more productively.

Every day I go into the gents bathrooms of bars and cafés and restaurants and on the walls put up pictures of her, with the question, 'Have You Had Intercourse With This Woman In The Last 24 Months?' There is room for signatures, and I leave pens there so that any men who have can sign it. I go back and check regularly and am quite fastidious about keeping accurate, detailed records of the results, as well as replacing pens and sheets for more signatures. More or less as expected, there's nearly a phone directory's amount of names that I've collected so far.

My counsellor told me that he meant yoga or salsa dancing, those kinds of hobbies, and certainly did not mean this, as though there was something very wrong with it.

"This is not very healthy, I'm afraid, and it won't lead to any closure," he said.

"I have to disagree," I answered, and told him I wouldn't be coming back and, as I was leaving, thanked him for all he had done in steering me, albeit unwittingly, in this direction.

"The truth is I've been feeling an incredible sense of purpose in my life in doing this important work," I explained. "It's so much more than a hobby now. I was never one to believe in destiny, but... Well, I really feel this might be mine."

Soup

It was pure dumb luck that I discovered my husband's affair with his secretary. They'd been meeting at hotels for months when he was supposed to be out of town. He'd always call and chat and tell me he loves me, so I never had cause to suspect anything was going on.

He either covered his tracks very well or I was blind to the evidence. I never noticed any incriminating lipstick on his collar, the way wives do in films.

It was such an ordinary day. I was preparing French onion soup the way my mother taught me to. I'd been cutting up a whole net of onions when I heard his key in the door and, as always, went to greet him there. With the excitement of him being home, I forgot to wipe away the tears that had been streaming down my face.

When I met him in the hall he saw my reddened, puffed-up eyes and soaking cheeks and a look of horror came over his face. Before I could explain, he threw himself at my feet and hugged my legs. He was weeping desperately himself then, and blubbering about how he never meant for any of this to happen, and how he was going to spend the rest of his life making it up to me if I could only forgive him.

Eventually, I was able to tell him I'd been chopping onions and hadn't really been crying, and he realised he'd made a terrible mistake. I'll never forget the look on his face. Any time I need a good laugh I remember it. All the pain of it aside, the look on his face was honestly the funniest thing I've ever seen.

Lesson

It was a quiet day at the restaurant where I work as a chef, so I got out much earlier than expected and was on my way home to fix a nice meal to surprise my wife after her tennis lesson. She had been working with a new trainer she described as a wizard, and her back-hand and serve were coming on leaps and bounds thanks to him.

When I arrived home I could hear a lot of oohing and ahhing coming from upstairs so went up to see what the racket was. I passed her favourite white pleated skirt at the top, and soon after passed a white tennis shirt that definitely did not belong to her. At this stage it was quite clear what was going on, so I removed my sharpest knife from my work bag.

It seemed to be quite the rally taking place but it came to a sudden stop when I kicked the door open. I lunged at him, brandishing the blade. My wife was screaming at me to stop but I ignored her, backing him into a corner. He soon passed out with the shock, which made it much easier to castrate him.

"New balls, please," I said, turning around to face her. I was really pleased with that one, so pleased that I very nearly started chuckling away there and then.

Gifts

I arrived home with a big bouquet of flowers and an expensive new gold bracelet and presented them to my wife. She was very excited about the unexpected gifts.

"What's the occasion?" she asked.

"The occasion is another day being married to the most wonderful woman in the world," I answered, taking her wrist in my hand and putting on the bracelet for her.

"I love it when you cheat on me," she said, giggling like a child on Christmas morning. "You always come home with the loveliest things for me. It's exquisite. I can't wait to show it off."

I was too shocked to even respond. She was right, of course, but I had no idea how she could have known and, evidently, she'd known all along. It turns out I didn't need to say anything, however, as she was far too engrossed in admiring her wrist and wasn't listening to any explanation I might be coming up with. So I said nothing and, instead, made myself useful, putting the flowers in some water.

Band

When I first told my girlfriend I was a musician, she couldn't hide her glee. I told her of my plans to make albums and tour the world and play famous venues, hoping to impress her, which I could see it did.

"That was so, so amazing," she said excitedly after coming to a dingy bar to hear us play for the first time. "You're going to be the biggest band in music history."

I was falling for her and had started writing songs about love, about a beautiful woman, and it was her each time, and soon we had a big record deal because of them.

"What did I tell you about music history?" she said, but it wasn't with her usual enthusiasm. She actually seemed let down.

"I'll call you every night," I said, leaving to begin a big tour in promotion of the album we'd finished making.

"Don't say anything you don't mean," she answered crossly, and then began weeping. It wasn't long before she became very negative and insecure. "If you'd rather be off signing breasts right now, just say so," she snapped one evening. "I wouldn't want to keep you from all those adoring fans."

There was one show that was delayed starting and so finished a bit later than expected, but I called her straight after.

"Oh, how nice of you to take a break from your groupie orgy to talk to me," she hissed down the phone. She was so paranoid that I was sleeping with other women. I tried everything I could to reassure her but nothing ever worked.

None of it mattered without her to share it with, of course, and I was beginning to worry that I might lose her. I hated that all of this was making her so unhappy and so decided to give it all up. I quit the band and told the record company where they could stick their contract. I couldn't wait to surprise her with the news. I'd even already managed to secure a job in a factory that makes paint.

"You mean you're not in the band anymore?" she asked when I turned up at her door in my new workman's overalls. She didn't seem pleased at all. "I hope you're making a really bad joke," she went on, "because I'm only interested in guys in bands."

Zombie

It started out with some severe flaking of the skin, like a bad case of eczema. It wasn't immediately obvious that my wife had contracted a zombie virus, but soon after that I noticed the colour vanishing from her face and her skin turning cold to the touch, not to mention her words becoming indecipherable grunts and ghoulish moans.

On top of those symptoms, she was getting to be very bitey, to the point that I'd had no choice but to stop giving her a kiss before going out to work in the morning.

I will admit that I'd not always been a good husband. I'd had silly affairs many times. It was a time in my life I'm not at all proud of and would take back in a heartbeat if there was any way to. We survived those years, just. I dealt with the shame with subsequent years of rigid fidelity and cherishing the vows I had besmirched.

While those vows are very clear on death, I wasn't sure how they pertained to my wife's undeadness, but figured the best course of action was to carry on loving, honouring, having and holding as best I could, and see where it takes us.

It got more and more difficult, of course, despite my very best efforts to keep a room temperature that would minimise decomposition. I would apply her make-up every day, and had become quite skilled at doing so, but it could only go so far to mask the advances of the rotting of her flesh.

Most difficult of all to take, the excitement of making love was gone. Her hair was coming out in clumps, and when I dressed her up in revealing lingerie, it mostly revealed that her once sumptuous flesh had turned green and her bones were sticking out through it. For all my best efforts to believe her sexy, I couldn't do it anymore.

Her lips, once so luscious and alluring, had become terribly fissured and bloodied from all the biting. Felatio, naturally, was totally out of the question.

Eventually, I had to face facts. It could not work out, and none of this was fair to either of us. I was prolonging the inevitable. No amount of love would reverse the symptoms of the virus, and so I said my heartfelt goodbyes, and she spat and hissed and chewed at her restraints in response.

Just like in the Romero films, all that was left was to separate her head from the rest of her body, which I managed cleanly enough with the hedge clippers and, as best I could, give her a proper Christian burial in the back garden. For a finish, I planted a red rose bush on top, her favourite. Her name was Rose, and I remember her beautiful face in each of its flowers.

Gigolo

I've been paying handsome, desirable men to seduce my wife. I know that might sound very unusual. It isn't some bizarre fetish, don't worry. You see, I had a bit of a cock-up recently with my wedding vows. I've felt just awful about it since, really I have. The guilt is killing me, eating away at me from the inside like some carnivorous bacteria.

I thought of coming clean but then decided it would hurt her too much, and why should she have all that pain to contend with when it's me who is in the wrong? I decided it might be best to even the score, then move on, live the happiest of lives together, maybe laugh about this many years from now.

The problem now is that it's costing me a fortune. All these gigolos don't come cheap, let me tell you. All of them have failed miserably, have come back to me and said how lucky I am to have such a beautiful and faithful wife as she. She told each one in no uncertain terms that she was happily married and they were wasting their breath.

I suppose I should be delighted about that. In normal circumstances, I'm sure I would be. However, the guilt just seems to be growing worse and worse. I could have been spending all this money taking her on the amazing holiday she deserves.

I decided I'd try one more, just one. He's very expensive, this guy, but has guaranteed me it will be done. He was so sure of it he said he wouldn't take a penny if it isn't. I've a good feeling about him. It's getting quite late and she's not home and hasn't called. It must be going well. I can feel it. Everything's going to be back to normal.

Understanding

We really understand each other, my wife and I.

"Understanding, it's why our marriage is such a success," I tell her sometimes, and she always agrees enthusiastically.

"It's a healthy, twenty-first century marriage," she told several friends over dinner when one commented on how perfect we are together and asked what our secret was.

Just last night, I rolled over onto her with an erection, trying my best to aim it somewhere between her legs – a stab in the dark, as they say – but she was having none of it.

"No, no," she cried out, "you'll just have to handle that yourself."

"Are you sure you're not in the mood?" I asked, hoping she might change her mind.

"Yes, I'm afraid so," she said, and there was something in her voice that let me know she was deeply sorry not to be able to help. "The guy from last night was very well endowed. I think I might be sore for the next few days. You understand, don't you, love?"

She does that a lot, says love at the ends of her sentences to me. It's one of those little things that always makes me think about how lucky I am.

"Of course I do, dear," I said as soothingly as I could. "I hope I didn't wake you."

Bust

My husband is out of the house every Tuesday evening for a sculpting class. I was delighted when he first told me about it. I thought of how I could have the girls over for wine and tapas without having to worry about him walking around in his underwear. He came home from the first class and proudly presented me with a wonky ash-tray. It was very sweet.

A pair of matching coffee cups and a vase followed, as well as a decorative archway for the aquarium. Then, some months into the classes, he arrived home with a bust which was, very literally, a bust.

"Where do you think you're going with that?" I asked him.

"I thought it would be nice on the dresser," he answered. That's where it is now, taunting me every day. It's the last thing I see before turning out the light and the first thing I notice each morning. I don't know why they had to be so large. I don't know why he couldn't have sculpted a modest, sensible pair of breasts more like my own.

I don't think I'll ever fully recover from the sight of him standing in front of the dresser, his hands on his hips, admiring it as though it were a successful end to a plumbing effort and not another woman's excessively endowed chest.

"Aren't I getting really good?" is what he had to say to me when he noticed me in the doorway, watching on in disbelief.

Boomerang

I know now I should have been more forgiving than I was. When my Aussie boyfriend swore it would never happen again, I should have believed him. I should at least have given him the chance to earn back my trust.

"She was nothing but a one-time drunken mistake," he said. "It didn't mean anything. Please, we can work this out. I can fix this." Pain and pride stopped me, however.

I know that to be the truth now. He would have fixed it. I wonder if he misses me the way I miss him, if he has this same burning in his chest. It's killing me, waiting to hear back from him. He really should have received my gift by now, a life-size cuddly koala, because that's what I used to call him: My Cuddly Koala Bear. It's the cutest thing. He even has a boomerang on his back and on it, I've stitched the message: Please, Please Come back!

Arrangement

My wife suggested we make our marriage more interesting – a bit more twenty-first century was the way she put it. Not knowing exactly what she meant by that, I pretended I did and foolishly agreed with her.

"Any successful, lasting marriage in this day and age, you can bet is down to open-mindedness," she explained. "All the divorces you hear about involve people stuck in a 1950s mentality, you can be sure of that."

"Yes, of course," I said, suddenly getting the impression that if I didn't agree she might insist on getting a divorce.

She has been entertaining a lot of young men in our bed lately while I'm outside, sitting on the couch and looking at the hands on the clock turning. Now and again she'll come out to refill a bottle of water, and I'll quickly hide the tears I've been crying and force myself to smile at her.

"Isn't this new arrangement of ours wonderful?" she asked a few days ago, and I agreed, and then she went back inside and closed the door, and the banging on the walls and moaning and dirty talk started up again.

Sometimes she even asks me to go out to the shop and get condoms or lubrication for her, which of course I agree to do very enthusiastically, worried that if I don't she might tell me I'm stuck in a 1950s mentality.

The hardest part is making small talk with her lovers when they come out of our bedroom, whether to fix a sandwich or some other reason. They all think I'm so fine with the arrangement that there's not even a need to put on pants. Many of them won't even wait a few minutes for their erection to go down.

8

"He wondered for the first time whether his faithfulness as a husband had been a matter of deliberate choice, or passive acquiescence. Had he deliberately suppressed the appetites of a potential philanderer for the sake of a greater happiness, or had his life taken the shape it had because he didn't have those appetites in the first place?"

James Lasdun
from 'The Natural Order' in
It's Beginning to Hurt

Same

We had a frank and teary conversation, trying to come to some sort of resolution. We couldn't go on the way we were. We agreed everything should be out in the open.

We were equally guilty, it turns out. No one will have the upper hand as we give getting back on track our best shot. We were both cheating, sorry liars but dead set now on giving monogamy a decent go.

"I'm glad there are no more secrets," I said, looking into her big, wet blue eyes.

"Me too," she replied, squeezing my hand.

"I don't want to make any promises, of course, but I'm feeling pretty good about never letting this happen again," I said earnestly, pulling her to me and feeling the pulsing beat of her heart.

"I was just about to say the same thing," she answered.

Massage

I was the most faithful husband ever, not even looking at other women. I fully deserved my wonderful wife's unending trust. Then the doctor told me I was suffering from stress.

"It isn't serious yet, luckily," he said. "Have you ever thought about going for a massage?" He recommended a place he had been to a few times, saying they performed miracles of relaxation and tension release on him.

From the first moment she put her hands on me I felt both awful and exhilarated. It was quite intimate, candles flickering, fragrant oils burning, gentle piano music. I felt its wrongness but also knew that I'd never tell her to stop what she was doing. Even when she moved her hands up the insides of my slicked thighs and I felt the first little twitch, I knew I should and yet couldn't end it there.

"Does it feel good?" she asked, her Thai accent stretching out all the syllables. She knew. She saw it twitch and was letting me know she saw it and that it was okay. I think she was encouraging the arousal.

I told myself I'd never go back but before too long I was dialling the number, booking my next appointment and requesting the same masseuse. I'm completely addicted now. I've had eleven of them, and count down days to the next appointment.

"Does it feel good?" she continues to ask, knowing the answer already.

"Yes, very good," I answer.

At some point I will have to confess. She deserves the truth. Her trust has never failed, but I don't deserve it anymore. After each time up on that table, the guilt weighs heavier and heavier. I get so stressed out thinking about how I'm going to tell her that soon enough I need to make another appointment in order to destress. I just can't help thinking the worst. I really don't see all of this having a happy ending.

Watch

Christmas was just around the corner and I was keeping an eye out for a new gold watch for my husband. I went from jewellery store to jewellery store, determined to find the most perfect piece.

When I saw it behind the glass, I knew it was the one and the search could finally end. I told the sales assistant that it was beyond perfect and she looked overjoyed for me, most likely thinking of her commission.

"I'll actually take two," I told her excitedly.

"Of course," she answered, and set about boxing them up inside fancy velvet cases. Thinking I couldn't possibly find something nearly as nice for my boyfriend, I thought it right to get him the same thing. I know some people might see it as just laziness, and some might even feel it cheapens the gesture (when I can assure you the gesture was not cheap), but the last thing I'd want is to favour one over the other.

List

Bless his heart, my husband is out there about to start painting the front of the house for me. He's been having an affair, I found out, and now I'm pretending to be furious and broken-hearted. I can see he is feeling awful about it. How could I ever have betrayed you like this, his eyes seem to say.

When he asked me if he'd ever be able to have my trust again I told him there was a small chance of it — that it was possible.

"That's wonderful," he said.

"It won't be easy," I warned him.

"No," he said, "but I'll do whatever it takes."

I started compiling a list immediately then of things that urgently needed doing. I handed it to him and said if he did everything on it I'd know that he was really serious about having my trust back. He grasped it enthusiastically from my hand and got straight to work.

The front of the house really is in a bad state. It's desperate. I'm mortified every time I look at it, so in that sense it's a good thing he had this affair.

I can't wait until everything on the list is done and I can tell him that I've been having an affair as well — that's if I can keep a straight face for that long.

Cherish

Maybe it had something to do with growing up knowing my father had done a runner before I'd been born, along with years of seeing my mother weeping endlessly and slugging from vodka bottles, but all I ever wanted was one man to love and cherish and spend the rest of my life with, and I believed truly that he was out there.

When I met him at long last, I knew I'd found happiness forever. I could endure any hardship or calamity that came my way once I knew he was there by my side, supporting me, squeezing my hand.

However, I just can't seem to stop meeting men I want only to love and serve and worship. If I go out to the shop to pick up cigarettes there'll be another one there, picking up gum or milk or a magazine. We'll both feel the chemistry and so he'll start making conversation and I'll start thinking how this is the man I'm destined to marry and I'll have to add him to my collection of wonderful men. It happens all the time.

I suppose I do know I'm supposed to just have one but I can't help it – I just can't bear to part with any. They are all so special and I want each and every one for myself because I believe no one else is capable of loving them and treasuring them and revering them the way I know I can, and forever. All my friends tell me I'm being very selfish but they obviously just don't get it. They clearly don't have anywhere near as much love to give as I have.

Pretzel

I found a wallet of DVDs. They'd been hidden. I had no doubt about it. I was never meant to find these.

They had no titles other than dates, written in black marker. Curious about them, I played them, not really expecting anything in particular. They turned out to be sextapes, every one of them.

I passed hours there, watching my husband and his ex-wife making love. I've never seen such contortionism, even at the circus. She kept folding her body up into the maddest positions I've ever seen. It was like she was doing impressions of various kinds of pretzel.

Eventually, I had watched them in full. Sometimes, I was so impressed that I forgot my horror and became aroused. They were exceptional performances, in all fairness. No one could say that they weren't.

I felt betrayed, of course. He had kept them all this time, and in doing that he had kept her all this time as well.

I consoled myself with the knowledge that in other ways I am the superior wife. My cooking is easily the best my husband has ever had. He has often joked about how his ex-wife didn't even know how to turn on the stove. Some of the tapes were filmed in the kitchen and there never seemed to be anything in the oven, although there was that one time when she turned herself into a dessert with a can of whipped cream.

Thoughts

They were sitting over breakfast at the kitchen table.

"Do you ever have thoughts about other women?" she asked him.

"Never," he lied, chewing on a piece of toast, and with not a moment's hesitation. "Why do you ask?"

"Oh, no reason," she answered, and sprinkled some salt on her eggs.

"Do you ever have fantasies about other men?" he asked.

"Oh yes, all the time," she responded, quite matter-of-factly. "I was just having them now, in fact, and I guess that's why it occurred to me to ask you. I suppose I was kind of hoping you had similar thoughts. I've no intention of stopping having them, but I could really do without the guilt I feel from time to time."

Pact

When I received an email from the only woman I ever loved it was approaching a decade since our last contact.

"I'm just not ready to settle down," she'd said back then. I knew she meant there were many more men she wanted to be able to sleep with first. I did get her to agree to a pact, however – that in ten years we'd discuss giving things another shot. I had hope. Difficult as it was, I spent several years hoping she was sleeping with as many men as possible, getting it out of her system. I wanted nothing more than for her to be ready to settle down to a more traditional life with me.

She was more beautiful than I remembered as she entered the café. All those old feelings I had for her burst there and then to the surface again. She hugged me and kissed my cheek, announcing to all present that it was wonderful to see me after all these years.

Then, about fifteen minutes or so into our big reunion, her phone rang.

"Sorry, I should really take this," she said, tapping the answer icon. When she was done with the call, she flashed a big smile, the one I always worshipped, across the table at me and my heart skipped several beats the way it used to do.

"My husband," she sighed, "just reminding me to pick up dog food and milk on the way home. Now then, where were we?"

"Um… We were about to discuss giving things another go between us," I said.

"Oh yes," she answered enthusiastically. "So… Is that something you'd still be interested in doing?"

Respond

My husband messaged me a picture of his private parts. It confirms what I've known for a long time, because I'm fully sure the picture was not meant for me. He definitely only sent it to me by mistake. I imagine whoever it was meant for might have received a message with a list of groceries to pick up from the supermarket. That would be more like one that was meant for me. I wasn't sure at first how to respond and took a little time to consider the possibilities. I decided against confronting him angrily, saw no point in it. I could have demanded he end the affair, or threatened divorce, or simply kicked him hard in the face, any number of things, but in the end decided to go into a bathroom cubicle at the café I was in, hitch up my dress, pull down my undies, take a picture of my own privates, and send it to him. I'm only sorry I couldn't see the look on his face when he realised what must have happened.

Geeky

I still don't know how to make sense of it. Suddenly I was pulling in to McDonald's for a Big Mac on the way home, then flirting with the geeky kid behind the counter, then taking his phone number, and finally blowing a seductive kiss at him as I backed out the door.

He couldn't have been any more than nineteen. At forty-three, happily married to a very successful paediatrician, I enjoy an enviable lifestyle, want for nothing. I don't ever do things like this. I'd like to explain what's come over me but don't know where to begin. Skinny, pale, excruciatingly awkward, he had the saddest little face I've ever seen.

He seemed so petrified by my attention, his pathetic little voice quivering while calling out the digits. It made me want him even more. I don't think I ever wanted anyone so badly. Even now, I just want to take him in my arms, tell him to weep, tell him it's going to be okay. I want to kiss every one of his oozing pimples and tell him he's gorgeous.

Elephant

Up until the wedding, my wife was in the gym daily but afterwards always had an excuse not to go. She was bringing home giant crisp packets, ice cream tubs and bars of chocolate all the time. It was so unlike her, but all my married friends just made these knowing faces when I told them about it.

When she discovered I'd been messing around with another woman I'd met at the gym, she was despondent.

"How can you risk throwing away all of this?" she asked. I did my best not to snigger. "What is it? Do you not find me attractive anymore?"

It was time to be honest, no sugar coating it for her. "You know I love you," I answered, "but you've turned into an elephant since we got married. It's as if you don't even care about how you look anymore."

She left me, and at first I was relieved. I had a brand new bachelor pad and there was no more finding half-eaten *Subway* sandwiches under the couch.

Months passed, though, and I was missing her terribly. Each day I'd think about how if she'd multiplied in size again, I'd still want her back more than anything, and think myself the luckiest man in the world to have her.

When I finally worked up the courage to tell her so, I found her back to her old, tight-bodied, beautiful self. She whipped her hair over her shoulder as she approached me, the way she used to. I pleaded and begged but she wasn't having any of it. She just kept smiling and twirling around so that I could appreciate every hypnotic angle of her.

"Everything can go back to the way it used to be," I tried one last time.

"I'm afraid not," she answered. "As they say, an elephant never forgets." Just then a fancy sports car pulled up and she hopped into it. It sped off and must have gone from zero to ninety in under three seconds. I suppose she just couldn't get away from me fast enough.

Grave

Unfortunately, my first husband didn't quite turn out to be the man of my dreams. Right up until I married him, sure enough, he was perfectly gentle, romantic and sweet. Every day after, I lived with a terrible, crippling fear. I didn't listen when good friends told me he was a vile, odious brute. I was sure they were just trying to take my happiness away, steal it for themselves.

"Over my dead body," he said to me when I screwed up the courage, at last, to ask for a divorce. It became his catch phrase after that. Everything and anything I might have wanted was always over his dead body, and he'd say the words with such a snarl. He was always jealous, quick tempered and violent. Maybe it was all the anger and hatred that caught up with him. I'm no doctor, but that stuff isn't good for the heart, I'd expect.

The day I married my second husband was the second best day of my life. We'd waited so patiently for that awful man to die. The best day, however, would have to be when I took my new husband to visit my first husband's grave. It was a summer's night and the stars were all out and we were quite merry after sharing a bottle of bubbly, and then the idea just popped into my mind. I put some music on with his phone and we danced there on the soft grass of the grave, over his dead body. We laughed giddily over his dead body. We got very carried away, and before too long were lying down, making love over his dead body.

9

"Undoubtedly I loved the very illicitness of it, of my wife sleeping nearby and knowing nothing of what I was doing."

Richard Ford
from 'Privacy' in
A Multitude of Sins

Hospital

for Ali Whitelock

I went to see my girlfriend at the hospital. I'd received a call to say there'd been a terrible car accident, which she caused after drinking half a bottle of *Jägermeister*.

"It's really a miracle that she has survived at all," the doctor I spoke to said.

A nice nurse took me to a small waiting room where there was another man claiming to be her boyfriend. I could see he was desperately worried. He was pacing the floor, so I did the same. I thought I might get to read the newspaper, but the sports section under my arm would have to wait.

When they let us in we both gasped at the sight of her. She was laid out in a near-complete body cast. The only part of her that we could see was a very horrified and guilty looking little face.

"Don't worry, we're not mad," I said.

"Just focus on resting," he said.

Later on, she said she saw her future flash in her mind when the car hit the other car and then ricocheted into the streetlamp. I wasn't in that future, she told me, her face full of sympathy for me, but he was.

She began describing to us in detail how patient he was in her vision, spooning puree into her mouth while she dribbled it down her chin. It sounded beautiful, like a scene from a movie that's going to clean up at the Oscars. They sounded so very in love. I sincerely wished them all the best, and told her I'd never forget her, then left, my sports section still tucked under my arm. My team had had a big win and I couldn't wait to read all about it.

Tattoo

My fiancée, who is quite a renowned tattoo artist, suggested that instead of traditional wedding rings, we get our wedding bands tattooed on. She seemed very excited about the idea and grabbed a sketchpad she had in front of her.

"Look at these," she said. "They are some of the designs I've been working on. Aren't they beautiful?"

"Wow, they really are," I answered, quite genuinely impressed by them, "but I'm not sure, my love. It's not very traditional, is it? What will our parents think?"

"They'll be okay with it. Besides, this way we can't ever lose our rings, nor can they be stolen, nor can we ever take them off because we've had a silly argument," she went on. "It'll be perfect."

"I see what you mean," I said. In fairness, she had made some good points. "Give me some time to think about it, just a few days, and I'll get back to you. Okay?" I was trying my utmost to come across calmly but was very concerned. I had to come up with a good way out of this. A tattoo wedding band would make things so much trickier picking up other women in hotel bars when away on business.

Honesty

My last girlfriend used to complain all the time that I could never be trusted to tell the truth, and with good reason. I really couldn't be trusted.

"You're a filthy liar," she'd often spit, and would sometimes throw something as well.

"That's not true," I'd protest, and put on what I hoped was a very trustworthy expression.

It didn't work out, of course, but then how can it without trust? I got a new girlfriend, and she just so happened to be deaf. She's absolutely fantastic. She is very understanding as well, doesn't fly into rages and throw things like my old girlfriend used to do. No, she's gentle and loving to no end.

We are very happy together, of course. I can't get enough of her smiling face, and the way she looks at me as though she has all she has ever wanted from this life. And I've improved so much at the whole honesty thing. I tell her the complete truth, in fact. I'm being serious, I really do. Each night, after I turn out the light – because she's a wonderful lip reader – I confess every little indiscretion, and each and every morning she kisses me and I know all has been forgiven.

Silly

Everyone was talking about the meteorite the experts said was heading straight for us, about to blast us into extinction. There was nothing we could do about it. Cherish the remaining time with those you love was their message to all.

"It will never happen," my husband said. "These so-called experts are always on about some disaster that's about to wipe us out. It never happens. Life goes on. Now go to sleep."

His words were no comfort. The hours were counting down to the time. All I could think about was that message. It has always been my husband's best friend I've loved, but he was already married. When I said 'yes' and then 'I do' it was only to keep him close.

"I know you're worried about it, but you'll feel very silly later when nothing happens," my husband said, and kissed my cheek and left for work.

My mind was made up. I was finally going to admit my true feelings. If the world was going to be blown to smithereens, I was determined for my last hours to be the greatest of flings with the man I've spent all these years wanting more than anything.

I went to his office immediately and told him straight out of my love for him, and said that if he feels the same we must spend these last hours together doing the things we've deprived ourselves of all these years.

Unfortunately, he assured me that he loved his wife very much, and that all this end of the world business was nonsense, while looking very ill-at-ease behind his desk. When I began undoing the buttons of my blouse seductively, hoping I could change his mind, he called for security, and two very large men came and escorted me out of the building.

I went home and sat and waited for the meteorite, eagerly anticipating it. It really couldn't strike the Earth quick enough as far as I was concerned. When I heard my husband's car pull into the driveway, though, I knew it just wasn't going to be my day. He was right, the world wasn't ending, life would go on, and I was feeling very, very silly.

Choose

Women's golf is putting a big strain on our relationship. It's the most bizarre thing. It was on the telly one evening and suddenly I couldn't take my eyes off it. I've been hooked ever since. I've never played golf or had any interest in it in the past, but now when my girlfriend tells me to change the channel I just turn up the volume until she leaves the room.

I tried watching men's golf and, as I feared, it did nothing for me. I spoke to a friend about it, but he just told me all female golfers are lesbians. I haven't been deterred, though. If anything, I've just been craving it more; more of their awful outfits, their powerful fairway strides, their crouches on the green, their tips of their caps to applauding galleries.

I tried watching women's tennis. I could plainly see they were beautiful and alluring, but the effect just wasn't the same. Female volleyball didn't do it for me either. I even watched women's gymnastics and felt nothing. Only female golfers seemed to fill me with that strange desire. My girlfriend thinks I'm as good as cheating on her. She won't put up with it anymore. She has told me I have to choose. I really do love her dearly, but I just can't help thinking women's golf would never give me an ultimatum like this.

Gynaecologist

My wife was very excited, on our first date, to discover I was a doctor.

"What kind of doctor?" she asked, but when I said I was a gynaecologist I couldn't help but notice the please-tell-me-you're-joking look she got on her face. Nevertheless, she said yes when I asked if we would have a second date, and she said yes again when I got down on one knee two years later.

Year after year of marriage and she has never grown any more comfortable with what I do for a living, which has also been her living all these years, paying for her expensive lunches and designer shoes and dresses.

"So, is that what you're doing all day, is it?" she snarled one evening as my head was between her thighs. I drew back, stunned and speechless at first.

"You visit a gynaecologist from time to time," I answered eventually. "Is this what happens when you do?" She didn't at all like the good sense in that and so stood up and stormed out of the room, slamming the door behind her.

There isn't much more I can do, only keep repeating myself, keep reassuring her every time she brings up her issues with my line of work. So, as patiently and understandingly as I can, that's what I do.

"It's just a job, dear, nothing more. I never take any pleasure in it," I lie.

Doubts

I'm ecstatic to be able to say I'll never be unfaithful to my husband. It hasn't been for want of trying, but everyone I've ever chanced has been so adamant in saying no. Some laughed hysterically at the idea, while others recoiled in apparent horror at the notion, while one man actually made the sign of the cross with his fingers as though in hope it might repel me, which I suppose it did. Whatever their means of showing it, they were all quite sure of their disinterest. So much rejection has given me incredible reassurance that my husband really, really loves me. I've had my doubts in the past, but I won't ever make that mistake again.

Lingerie

Our love life had been diminishing for quite some time. The spark was gone and I was looking at other women and imagining extramarital liaisons with them.

My wife, always the proactive one, went out to the *Ann Summers* shop and bought an array of new lingerie, presumably thinking to seduce me. She arrived home with the bags proudly displayed and began pulling frilly this and sequined that out onto the kitchen table, where I was trying to eat a roast beef sandwich.

I had to hand it to her, though – her choices were inspired. It all looked very sexy indeed. She started saying something or other but it was too late, I was far too distracted by then with imagining my secretary wearing each piece. She isn't very good at her job, fails to perform even basic secretarial duties, but in my imagination she does everything I ask of her, and takes no sick days.

Duck

The phone beeped and vibrated on the desk. A text had come through from my husband.

"I can't go on with the deception," it read. "I hope you won't hate me, but unfortunately I'm married. I have a wife. I hope this won't change anything between us, but I'll understand if it does." He's a terror for sending messages to the wrong person.

"Yes, I'm well aware that you're married," I texted back. "I think that text might have been meant for someone else, LOL. Anyway, I should be home around six. I'm making your favourite, duck à l'orange. See you later."

Muscles

I had joined the gym and after a couple of months was feeling quite good about myself. I had lost some weight and the muscle definition in my arms and legs and chest was showing and people had been remarking on the difference. My confidence, naturally, was coming on in leaps and bounds. My insecurities were fading away with each passing day.

One afternoon, as I was using a rowing machine, a beautiful girl on a treadmill caught my eye. She had been looking at me admiringly, I noticed, and she smiled a very alluring smile in my direction. Almost miraculously, I was able to return the smile, and so we were smiling back and forth at one another for some time then from our respective exercise machines. She had a really wonderful body, and I started thinking about how we might go out together, and kiss and, after a suitable time, have sex, and it could be really fit, hard-bodied sex, no flab between us, no hang-ups, no love handles.

I stole many glances at her tensing muscles, legs and arms, and knew if she turned around she would have a bum to die for. You can always tell, after all. I saw the rise and fall of breast in her sports bra and was getting carried away like a child on Christmas Eve surveying all the shiny packages beneath the tree, greedy and impatient to unwrap them all.

Then a man entered and took off his jumper to reveal ridiculously large biceps. He positioned himself in front of a mirror not far from us, and proceeded to do seemingly endless repetitions of the most colossal weights that must have been heavier than me, and hardly a strain ever showed on his face.

She was looking at him then and I knew it was over between us. What we had was gone and I felt the squeeze of the loss in my chest. I knew she wouldn't look in my direction again, wouldn't smile at me that way again and, sure enough, she didn't. She just kept looking at him and his freakish Dwayne Johnson muscles. She was leering so obviously there were even a few moments when she came close to falling from her treadmill. I kept looking her way, though, willing her eyes back to mine, futilely. He never once looked at her during all of this, didn't even notice her steamy gaze. He was far too engrossed in lifting his weights up and down, over and over again in the mirror. He only had eyes for his reflection, with which, anyone could see, he had fallen hopelessly in love.

Nature

It all began when she picked up a book about getting back to Nature. That's how she described it – getting back to Nature – and I could feel the capital N in the way she said it. It was just little things for a while, so I wasn't concerned, but then she was doing all sorts of funny things, like hugging and kissing trees, or having conversations with insects, things you'll draw very queer looks for.

"You should join me," she'd say, whenever she'd catch me arching an eyebrow. Then one day she told me she was going to give up wearing clothes. She put them all in big bags and nakedly brought them around to the charity stores.

I went along with it, feeling sure enough it wouldn't be long before she changed her mind. After all, it's not exactly the Bahamas we're living in. I can't really say if she noticed the mayhem she was causing, serious car crashes, people walking into poles, not to mention all the very sudden erections in the streets. She's very beautiful, you see, and goes to the gym, and does Pilates in the garden. I'm not much of a humanitarian, so I could get over people being killed in tragic accidents, walking out in front of buses and the like. It was the feeling that I was sharing her with the undeserving world that really irked me.

Selfie

I've tried very hard to stop looking at my girlfriend's *Facebook* page so obsessively. For all my best efforts, I think I might actually be cyber stalking her. I check every new selfie upload, every comment. She's really gone mad into posting those selfies, pouty faces and jacked up cleavage and 'fuck me eyes' all painted up. I don't understand it at all.

"Everyone is doing it," is all she says on the matter, then steps in close to me, taking a selfie with me next to her, which she then uploads to *Facebook* but without referring to me as her boyfriend.

All these guys I don't know and have never met nor heard her mention are commenting on her selfies and leaving lines of x's after them.

"They're just friends," she says when I try asking questions. "It's called having a laugh. You should really try it some time." She 'likes' their comments and answers them with more lines of x's.

She has informed me that I'm turning into one of those jealous, paranoid boyfriends and that I should really do something about that.

"It's not attractive at all," she assured me. I could see her point. I'm sure it isn't, so I have decided to trust her completely. Today, I'm going to promise her, is the first day of a new and improved me.

About Edward O'Dwyer

Edward O'Dwyer was born in Limerick, Ireland, in 1984, where he currently lives. To date, he has written two collections of poetry – *The Rain on Cruise's Street* (Salmon Poetry, 2014) and *Bad News, Good News, Bad News* (Salmon Poetry, 2017).

O'Dwyer's work has featured in many journals and anthologies worldwide, including *The Forward Book of Poetry*, and has been nominated regularly for *Forward*, *Pushcart* and *Best of the Web* prizes. 'The Whole History of Dancing' won the 'Best Single Poem' award at the Eigse Michael Hartnett Festival in 2018.

In 2010 O'Dwyer was selected by Poetry Ireland for their Introductions Series. He has been shortlisted for a Hennessy Award for 'Emerging Poetry', and on three occasions for the North West Words Prize.

O'Dwyer has also edited two anthologies of poetry for Limerick community publisher Revival Press – *Sextet* (2010) and *Sextet 2* (2016).

Cheat Sheets is his first book of fiction, for which he is already working on a sequel. A third collection of poetry is due in 2020, again from Salmon Poetry.

Thanks

I would look to thank Truth Serum Press for believing in this manuscript, and to thank Matt Potter for helping me to improve it during editing.

I would like to thank Dan Rhodes for all of his books. I just want more books like these to exist. This is my attempt.

I would lastly like to thank the two women at the next table to me one day in a café in Limerick talking loudly about the affair one was having. I was looking for the right theme for this kind of book. Your contribution is huge.

Acknowledgements

I would like to extend my gratitude to the editors of the following, in which some of the stories, or versions of them, were previously published:

Danse Macabre
Headstuff
The Cabinet of Heed
Stanzas Journal
Dodging the Rain

Also from TRUTH SERUM PRESS

https://truthserumpress.net/catalogue/

 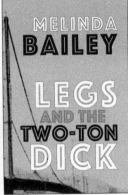 

- *The Crazed Wind* by Nod Ghosh
  978-1-925536-58-4 (paperback) 978-1-925536-59-1 (eBook)
- *Legs and the Two-Ton Dick* by Melinda Bailey
  978-1-925536-37-9 (paperback) 978-1-925536-38-6 (eBook)
- *Square Pegs* by Rob Walker
  978-1-925536-62-1 (paperback) 978-1-925536-63-8 (eBook)

- *On the Bitch* by Matt Potter
  978-1-925536-45-4 (paperback) 978-1-925536-46-1 (eBook)
- *Kiss Kiss* by Paul Beckman
  978-1-925536-21-8 (paperback) 978-1-925536-22-5 (eBook)
- *Dollhouse Masquerade* by Samuel E. Cole
  978-1-925536-21-8 (paperback) 978-1-925536-22-5 (eBook)

Also from TRUTH SERUM PRESS

https://truthserumpress.net/catalogue/

- *Inklings* by Irene Buckler
  978-1-925536-41-6 (paperback) 978-1-925536-42-3 (eBook)
- *Too Much of the Wrong Thing* by Claire Hopple
  978-1-925536-33-1 (paperback) 978-1-925536-34-8 (eBook)
- *Track Tales* by Mercedes Webb-Pullman
  978-1-925536-35-5 (paperback) 978-1-925536-36-2 (eBook)

 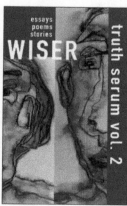 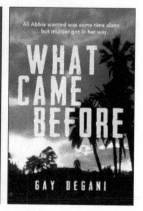

- *True Truth Serum Vol. #1*
  978-1-925536-29-4 (paperback) 978-1-925536-30-0 (eBook)
- *Wiser Truth Serum Vol. #2*
  978-1-925536-31-7 (paperback) 978-1-925536-32-4 (eBook)
- *What Came Before* by Gay Degani
  978-1-925536-05-8 (paperback) 978-1-925536-06-5 (eBook)

Also from TRUTH SERUM PRESS

https://truthserumpress.net/catalogue/

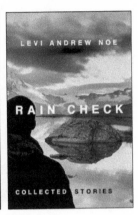

- *Hello Berlin!* by Jason S. Andrews
  978-1-925536-11-9 (paperback) 978-1-925536-12-6 (eBook)
- *Deer Michigan* by Jack C. Buck
  978-1-925536-25-6 (paperback) 978-1-925536-26-3 (eBook)
- *Rain Check* by Levi Andrew Noe
  978-1-925536-09-6 (paperback) 978-1-925536-10-2 (eBook)

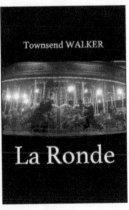

- *Luck and Other Truths* by Richard Mark Glover
  978-1-925101-77-5 (paperback) 978-1-925536-04-1 (eBook)
- *The Miracle of Small Things* by Guilie Castillo Oriard
  978-1-925101-73-7 (paperback) 978-1-925101-74-4 (eBook)
- *La Ronde* by Townsend Walker
  978-1-925101-64-5 (paperback) 978-1-925101-65-2 (eBook)